William Pitt, Charles Manners Rutland

Correspondence Between the Right Honble. William Pitt

and Charles, duke of Rutland, Lord Lieutenant of Ireland, 1781-1787. With

introductory note by John, duke of Rutland

William Pitt, Charles Manners Rutland

Correspondence Between the Right Honble. William Pitt
and Charles, duke of Rutland, Lord Lieutenant of Ireland, 1781-1787. With introductory note by John, duke of Rutland

ISBN/EAN: 9783337399344

Printed in Europe, USA, Canada, Australia, Japan

Cover: Foto ©Andreas Hilbeck / pixelio.de

More available books at **www.hansebooks.com**

CORRESPONDENCE

BETWEEN

THE RIGHT HONBLE. WILLIAM PITT

AND

CHARLES DUKE OF RUTLAND

LORD LIEUTENANT OF IRELAND

1781—1787

WITH INTRODUCTORY NOTE

BY

JOHN DUKE OF RUTLAND

WILLIAM BLACKWOOD AND SONS
EDINBURGH AND LONDON
MDCCCXC

INTRODUCTORY NOTE.

So much has been said and written during the discussions on Home Rule in praise of Grattan's Parliament, and in condemnation of Mr Pitt's conduct in abolishing it, that I have thought it right to give to the public the following correspondence between that statesman and my grandfather, the fourth Duke of Rutland.

The letters of the latter throw a vivid light on the conduct of the Irish Parliament, and on the prejudicial effect the factious and self-seeking spirit of its members had on the fortunes of the country.

Mr Montgomery Martin, indeed, nearly half a century ago, called attention to some of the more salient proofs of that misconduct; but his work is now not very accessible, and the story of Grattan's Parliament during these important years is best told in the confidential correspondence between the Prime Minister and the Lord Lieutenant.

How early and how strongly the necessity of a Union had impressed itself on the mind of the latter may be seen in his letter of June 16, 1784, and it may well be that sixteen years afterwards the prophecy of his friend may have been recalled to Mr Pitt's recollection. The letters on the subject of the proposed Commercial Union between the two countries show the impartial spirit which animated both the writers, and the factious conduct of Mr Grattan and Mr Flood, which led to the abandonment of that great measure, on which Mr Pitt had bestowed so much care and industry; while those on the prosecution of the Commercial Treaty with France testify to Mr Pitt's minute care for the interests of Ireland.

I have only to add that the motive which induced Lord Stanhope forty-eight years ago to omit a name having by lapse of time ceased to operate, I have published it, and that the footnotes, with one exception, are his.

RUTLAND.

Jan. 1890.

NOTE BY LORD MAHON

(*EARL STANHOPE*).

THE following correspondence between Mr Pitt
and Charles fourth Duke of Rutland was preserved by the Duchess his widow, after his
untimely decease in 1787, until her own in
1831, and was lately and unexpectedly found
by the present Duke in arranging her Grace's
papers.

The interest and importance of these letters,
together with the wish and recommendation of
several of his friends, have induced the Duke to
permit their appearance in a printed form, and
he has done me the honour of intrusting them
for that purpose to my care and revision.

In the performance of this welcome task, I
have selected every one of Mr Pitt's letters, and
a considerable number of the Duke's, which
throw great light on the state of parties in

Ireland, and incidentally display his own accomplished mind and honourable character. Neither
names nor expressions have been omitted from
the text (except in one instance, where it might
have given pain to several persons now alive),
and I have added only such few notes as I
thought necessary to its elucidation.

MAHON.

LONDON, *July* 1842.

CORRESPONDENCE

BETWEEN

MR PITT AND THE DUKE OF RUTLAND.

———•———

MR PITT TO THE DUKE OF RUTLAND.

LINCOLN'S [INN], *Friday, March* 9, [1781.]

MY DEAR DUKE,—You will, I am sure, have the goodness to admit Parliamentary engagements as an excuse for my not having thanked you for your letter as instantly as I wished. The favourable idea you have received of my first attempt [1] I must attribute to a partial reporter, and, what is yet more, a willing hearer. If, however, it has been in any degree successful, what effect should it have but to revive and increase, if possible, my sense of that friendship which has

---

[1] Mr Pitt's first speech in Parliament was delivered February 26, 1781, on Mr Burke's Bill for the Regulation of the Civil List.

A

enabled me to pursue the favourite objects of my mind? I cannot deceive myself with the thought of anything which relates to me being to penetrate, as you say, the obscurity of retirement, but much less can I bring myself to think of that retirement as applied to your Grace. Let me rather hope that I shall have the satisfaction of fighting under your banner in the cause to which we are alike attached, and of proving to the world how much I know the value and feel the honour of such a connection. I mean to leave town on Wednesday, if no particular business arises, in order to join the circuit. On my return, I hope I shall have the pleasure of seeing you in town.

My brother is probably with you by this time. It is necessary, for the peace of his conscience, to inform him, that the loss of a vote was not felt yesterday, as I expected, the Contractor's Bill not having been opposed. I flatter myself, the time may soon come when one vote may be of more consequence, as I think there is a great appearance of increasing vigour, and I do not despair of being summoned from the Land's End, to make part of a majority, before the circuit is over. May I beg my best respects to the Duchess. — Ever, with the truest attachment, sincerely yours, W. PITT.

MR PITT TO THE DUKE OF RUTLAND.

DOWNING STREET, *April* 30, [1782 ?]

MY DEAR DUKE,—You will probably have learnt that *Lord Scarborough is not dead,* and Lincoln not actually vacant. But before I had received your letter, a gentleman of the name of Turnor, who has connections in Lincolnshire, who had been strongly recommended to me some time since as a friend, went down to try his ground, in the expectation that the vacancy may soon take place. I do not know that Government has any direct interest at Lincoln that will signify for any candidate ; but I am so far committed to Mr Turnor by what passed before I knew that you had anything in contemplation, that I cannot encourage any one in opposition to him, if he stands. I have not seen Major Hobart, but will take the first opportunity of explaining to him these circumstances. I have not a moment to do more than thank you for your letters.—With every good wish, I remain, your affectionate and faithful friend, W. PITT.

MR PITT TO THE DUKE OF RUTLAND.

BERKELEY SQUARE,
Saturday, Nov. 22, [1783.]

MY DEAR DUKE,—I have been very near troubling you on the subject of Cambridge, on Mansfield's appointment; but the Duke of Grafton took fright, and prevented Euston's standing. The business in the House of Commons made it impossible for me. Either of us would, I am clear, have carried it; but as it has turned out, Mansfield is still triumphant. We are in the midst of contest, and I think approaching *to a crisis*. The bill which Fox has brought in relative to India will be, one way or other, decisive for or against the coalition. It is, I really think, the boldest and most unconstitutional measure ever attempted, transferring at one stroke, in spite of all charters and compacts, the immense patronage and influence of the East to *Charles Fox, in or out of office*. I think it will with difficulty, if at all, find its way through our House, and can never succeed in yours. Ministry trust all on this one die, and will probably fail. They have hurried on the bill so fast, that we are to have the second reading on Thursday next, *Nov. 27th*. I think we shall be strong on that day, but much stronger in the subsequent stages. If you have any member within fifty or a hundred miles of you, who cares for the constitution or the country, pray send him to the House of Commons as quick as you can. I trust you see that this bill will not easily reach the House of Lords; but I must tell you that ministry flatter themselves with carrying it through before Christmas. If that should grow probable, you will allow me to trouble you with another letter. Adieu.—Ever most faithfully yours,   W. PITT.

For fear of mistakes, I must tell you that I am at a house which my brother has taken here, and not at Shelburne House.

I do not see Lord Tyrconnel in town, nor *Pochin*, nor Sir Henry Peyton. Can you apply to any of them? They may still be in time for some of the stages of the bill.

MR PITT TO THE DUKE OF RUTLAND.

BERKELEY SQUARE,
Saturday Night, Dec. 6, [1783.]

MY DEAR DUKE,—A thousand thanks to you for your letter. I did not venture to answer your former by the post, trusting to see you so soon, but I received it perfectly safe. The closet will do everything, as far as I can judge, in fair co-operation and concert, *if* the crisis is found to be ripe, which I think it will. I am happy to hear you have filled your pockets so well with proxies; I hope your servant will bring them down in time, but at all events do not wait for them if it requires any time. They may follow you, but we cannot do without you here. Adieu.—Ever yours,   W. PITT.

MR PITT TO THE DUKE OF RUTLAND.

BERKELEY SQUARE, *Tuesday,* 11 *o'clock.*

MY DEAR DUKE,— In this decisive moment, for my own own sake, and that of the country, I trust I may have recourse to your zeal and friendship. My hands are so full that I cannot be sure of calling on you. Will you, if possible, come here at twelve. I am to see the King at one.[1]—Ever most truly yours,   W. PITT.

MR PITT TO THE DUKE OF RUTLAND.

BERKELEY SQUARE,
Tuesday Night, Feb. 17, [1784.]

MY DEAR DUKE,—Nothing passed of material consequence yesterday. The House came to

[1] In the new administration formed in December 1783, Mr Pitt was appointed Prime Minister, and the Duke of Rutland Lord Lieutenant of Ireland.

[The Duke was, in the first instance, Lord Privy Seal, which office he exchanged in 1784 for the Lord-Lieutenancy, at Mr Pitt's request.—R.]

resolutions relative to the proceedings of the Lords, which will not have much effect one way or other. The House, however, sat so late, that we adjourned till to-morrow; we shall then probably come to the question of postponing the supplies, though I think the enemy rather flinches. What the consequence will be is as doubtful as when you left us. At all events, I trust nothing can arise to interrupt your progress; for come what may, your taking possession is, I think, of the utmost consequence. I hope to be able to send you further account before you reach Holyhead. My brother has given me the memorandums you left, which must be managed as well as they can. The *independents* are still indefatigable for coalition, but as ineffectual as ever.—Believe me always, my dear Duke, most faithfully and affectionately yours,

W. PITT.

MR PITT TO THE DUKE OF RUTLAND.

[*Private.*]   BERKELEY SQUARE,
                    Tuesday Night, March 10, 1784.

MY DEAR DUKE,—I am happy more than I can tell you in all the good accounts you have sent us from Ireland. I ought long before this to have made you some return, but I could never have done it so well as this evening. We yesterday were beat only by *one*, on the con-

cluding measure of opposition, a long representation to the King, intended as a manifesto to
the public, where its effect is not much to be
dreaded. To-day, the Mutiny Bill has gone
through the committee, without any opposition (after all the threats), to the duration
for a twelvemonth. The enemy seem indeed to
be on their backs, though certainly the game
left in our hands is still difficult enough. They
give out that they do not mean to oppose supplies, or give any interruption to business; but
their object is certainly to lie in wait, or at least
catch us in some scrape that may make our
ground worse with the public before any *appeal*
is made there. The sooner that can be done
I think the better, and I hope the difficulties in
the way are vanishing. You see I am so full of
English politics that I hardly say a word on
Irish, though I am sure you have a right to expect a considerable mixture of them. Another
messenger will follow this in a day or two, and
I will then acquit my promise of sending the
paper Orde [1] left with me, with the necessary
remarks. In the meantime, I think there is
nothing in that paper on which any *immediate*
steps are to be proposed by Government, and I
trust from your accounts time will be allowed

[1] The Right Honourable T. Orde, appointed Secretary for
Ireland.

for deliberations; but no time shall be wasted in doing all we can on our present information. I am much obliged to Orde for the early account he gave me of your prosperous arrival. From some hand or other, pray let me hear of you as often as possible. I write now in great haste, and tired to death, even with victory, for I think our present state is entitled to that name. Adieu, my dear Duke.—With every wish for the happiness and honour you have so well earned a right to, and with the truest friendship and affection, believe me ever yours,

W. PITT.

MR PITT TO THE DUKE OF RUTLAND.

DOWNING STREET,
Tuesday Night, March 23, [1784.]

MY DEAR DUKE,—The interesting circumstances of the present moment, though they are a double reason for my writing to you, hardly leave me the time to do it. *Per tot discrimina rerum,* we are at length arrived within sight of a dissolution. The bill to continue the powers of regulating the intercourse with America to the 20th of June will pass the House of Lords to-day. That, and the Mutiny Bill, will receive the Royal Assent to-morrow, and the King will then make a short speech, and dis-

solve the Parliament. Our calculations for the
new elections are very favourable, and the
spirit of the people seems still progressive in our
favour. The new Parliament may meet about
the 15th or 16th of May, and I hope we may so
employ the interval as to have all the necessary
business rapidly brought on, and make the session a short one. I imagine you have settled
all your Parliamentary arrangements; but at
all events you will be in time to send any fresh
directions before the elections can come on.
The writs will bear teste Thursday the 25th.
Forgive my telling you how anxious all your
friends are that Pulteney should, if possible, be
disposed of some other way than by a seat in
Parliament; and yet I hardly know how it can
be done. The D. of Newcastle will positively
not bring in Ambler; but we will certainly take
care of him in the manner you wish. Lord
Hood's prospect in Westminster is very favourable. We shall also try Middlesex, and, I hope,
both the county and city of York. The prospect
in the two last places will depend principally on
the issue of the county meeting next Thursday,
which will be a hard-fought battle, though I
think we shall be victorious. This is enough of
English news to trouble you with at present.
I hope and trust everything goes on in Ireland
as favourably as it commenced. We shall now

soon have a little more leisure, and be better able to attend to real business in a regular way, instead of the occurrences of the day. I shall keep this letter open till evening, or perhaps to-morrow morning, and will write to you again as soon as possible.—Ever, my dear Duke, most truly and faithfully yours, W. PITT.

I shall stand for Cambridge, which is rather unexplored ground at present; but I am sanguine in my expectations, though I am afraid I shall feel your absence.

MR PITT TO THE DUKE OF RUTLAND.

DOWNING STREET, *April* 19, 1784.

MY DEAR LORD,[1]—The gentleman who will have the honour of delivering this letter to your Grace is Mr Harward, whom I took the liberty of mentioning to you before you left England. He is, I understand, related to Lord Grandison's family, with whom your Grace knows our connection. If it should be in your power to take him under your protection, I should be extremely obliged to you for any favour you will show him, of which I flatter myself you will

---

[1] This appears, from the change of style, to have been a formal letter of introduction sent open by Mr Harward.

find him not undeserving. His connections in
Ireland make him wish to be established in that
country, and will afford your Grace an opportunity to be more particularly informed concerning him, if you will.take the trouble to have
inquiries made.—I am, my dear Lord, your most
faithful and obedient servant,   W. PITT.

MR PITT TO THE DUKE OF RUTLAND.

DOWNING STREET, *April* 21, 1784.

MY DEAR DUKE,—I hope from the timely pre-
caution and vigilance you have employed against
the suspected attempts in Dublin you will have
completely frustrated the horrid effect of them,
and that anxiety on that subject is vanishing.
The idea is such as must leave one very solici-
tous, while any traces of it subsist; though I am
inclined to hope, from the particulars you have
sent, that the plan was not very deep-laid nor
deliberate. I rejoice with you most truly in approaching to the end of your session in so prosperous and honourable a manner. As we ap-
proach towards the opening of our campaign,
the prospect of being able to follow your example grows more and more confirmed. I shall
be happy to hear from you as fully and particularly as you can have the goodness to write,

whenever you can find the leisure. I do not wonder that neither of us is able to be quite so ample a correspondent as I think we both intended. With regard to Mr Preston, the canonry of Windsor was gone long before I received your letter, and three or four absolute engagements I am under that I do not think I can be released from. I should very much wish to know what you have in contemplation on the subject. You may be sure I shall be happy to obey your order the moment I can, though ecclesiastical preferment is the greatest plague I have, and it will be difficult to convince people that Ireland cannot find patronage for itself. I undertook very long since, but I am afraid forgot to mention to you, that I had learnt from Pratt,[1] the wishes of his brother-in-law, Mr Stewart, to be advanced to the Irish peerage whenever a creation takes place. His connection with Lord Camden, joined to what I hear of his situation and character, makes it a very desirable object that he should be gratified, whenever it can be done with propriety. You will understand that I have done no more than promise to favour his pretensions as far as may be proper, but have left everything to depend on the arrangements you may think proper to

[1] John Jeffreys Pratt, afterwards second Earl and first Marquess Camden.

make.   Indeed the whole subject of Irish peerages appears to me to be delicate, and requiring
much consideration.   This particular point I believe I mentioned to Orde before he left us, and
desired him to communicate it to you.   We
have no fresh news here, but from India, from
whence accounts are come within this day or
two, which look as if the peace with Tippoo
Saib would be secure, a point which has given
us some anxiety.   I have been exceedingly hurt
at the business of Leicester, all of which falls on
my shoulders, but which you will easily believe
was without my being aware of the circumstances.   In fact, however, I believe nothing
could have saved Booth Grey.   Pray give my
compliments to Mr Orde, and many thanks for
his letters.   Adieu.—Ever yours,   W. Pitt.

MR PITT TO THE DUKE OF RUTLAND.

Downing Street, *May* 24, 1784.

My dear Duke,—I cannot let the messenger
go without congratulating you on the prospect
confirmed to us by the opening of the session.
Our first battle was previous to the address, on
the subject of the return for Westminster.   The
enemy chose to put themselves on bad ground,
by moving that two members ought to have

been returned, without first hearing the High Bailiff to explain the reasons of his conduct. We beat them on this, by 283 to 136. The High Bailiff is to attend to-day, and it will depend upon the circumstances stated whether he will be ordered to proceed in the scrutiny, or immediately to make a double return, which will bring the question before a committee. In either case I have no doubt of Fox being thrown out, though in either there may be great delay, inconvenience, and expense, and the choice of the alternative is delicate. We afterwards proceeded to the address, in which nothing was objected to, but the thanking the King expressly for the dissolution. Opposition argued everything weakly, and had the appearance of a vanquished party, which appeared still more in the division, when the numbers were 282 to 114. We can have little doubt that the progress of the session will furnish throughout a happy contrast to the last. We have indeed nothing to contend with but the heat of the weather, and the delicacy of some of the subjects which must be brought forward. Adieu. May I beg my best respects and congratulations to the Duchess?—Ever faithfully and affectionately yours, W. PITT.

THE DUKE OF RUTLAND TO MR PITT.

[*Private.*]   DUBLIN CASTLE, *June* 16, 1784.

MY DEAR PITT,—It is with extreme satisfaction that I congratulate you on the success which has accompanied your very spirited exertions, in which, however, I must confess myself to be a little interested, as the effects of your decided victory will have a most material influence on my government and situation in this country.

Lord Mornington [1] informs me that he has had a conversation with you on Irish affairs, and by this time you will probably have communicated with Mr Orde on all the important questions which are likely to press, and on the different commercial points which remain unadjusted between Great Britain and Ireland. I hope the learned in trade may be able to strike out such regulations as may appease and conciliate the spirit of dissatisfaction and discontent which has obtained in this country, and at the same time not materially embarrass the commerce and manufactures of Great Britain. For my part, I pretend not to be competent to enter into any detail of the kind; but of this I can judge, that the circumstances and claims of Ireland are mat-

---

[1] Now Marquess Wellesley.

ters which at least require a serious investigation;
but that whatever advantages Great Britain may
be enabled and disposed to grant, let them be
declared to be *conclusive*. I must press this idea
on your mind as a point in any arrangement *indispensable*, for as long as anything indefinite
remains for expectation to feed upon, this country
will never be at peace. The question of reform,
should it be carried in England, would tend
greatly to increase our difficulties, and I do not
see how it will be evaded. In England it is a
delicate question, but in this country it is difficult and dangerous in the last degree. The views
of the Catholics render it extremely hazardous;
and though Lord Charlemont and Mr Flood seem
to exclude *them* from their ideas of reform, yet
in some late meetings, and in one particularly
held lately in this city, the point entirely ran on
their admission to vote, which was carried with
a single negative. Your proposition of a certain
proportionable addition of county members would
be the least exceptionable, and might not perhaps
materially interfere with the *system of Parliament* in this country, which, though it must be
confessed it does not bear the smallest *resem-
blance to representation*, I do not see how quiet
and good government could exist under any
more popular mode. Could the volunteers be
induced to disband, and return their arms to

Government, provided such a very temperate reform as you proposed should take place, it might perhaps be policy to concede something to their wishes, and, on moderate terms, the leading interests in Parliament might be prevailed upon to acquiesce.

The volunteer corps were reviewed in the Phœnix Park about a fortnight since. Their numbers were much diminished from the former year, in spite of all the exertions made use of to alarm and irritate, so that I am in hopes this self-appointed army may fall to the ground without the interposition of Government, which would prove a most fortunate circumstance. If some such event should not have effect, the period cannot be far distant when they must be spoken to in a peremptory and decisive manner. For the existence of a government is very precarious while an armed force, independent of and un-connected with the State, for the purpose of awing the Legislature into all its wild and visionary schemes, is permitted to endure. The northern newspapers take notice of an intention in some of the corps to address the French King, and which they recommend as a very proper and spirited measure. No meeting for such a *laudable* purpose has yet taken place. I can scarcely believe it, though the madness of some of these armed legislators might go to anything. Were

I to indulge a distant speculation, I should say
that without *an union* Ireland will not be connected with Great Britain in twenty years
longer.

The state of Europe seems to be peculiarly
complicated and embarrassing. If the designs of
the Emperor, together with the intrigues of the
French and the Dutch, should be productive of
war, it may perhaps be difficult for England to
avoid being eventually engaged in it; though I
have the greatest confidence in your prudence
and address to obviate so ruinous a contingency.
Under the possibility, however, of such an event,
I cannot entirely assent to the policy of reducing
the army at this moment. In this country it
may generate very unpleasant effects. It is impossible to foresee how far the spirit of the volunteers may be raised by the prospect of but a
small military force, or to what new objects they
may direct their attention. Ireland is not a land
of tranquillity, nor can Government be maintained
respectable, unless it be prepared for all contingencies. As far, therefore, as the reduction relates
to this country, I must protest against it; but if
the measure is founded on motives too powerful,
and is too far decided upon to be retracted, I
hope you will send us some substitute for the
force we are to be deprived of. In any case,
however, you may be assured, that neither my

zeal, nor, I trust, my firmness, will suffer any diminution.

I do not comprehend the ministerial changes which are reported to be taking effect. Is Lord Carmarthen to go to Paris? and why? And who is to be Secretary of State? How do you dispose of the Duke of Dorset? I hope no alteration will be made in the home department. I should be much concerned to lose Lord Sydney; he makes my situation very pleasant, and is a most practicable, punctual, and good-humoured correspondent. It astonishes me that in the triumphant career of your affairs you have found no successor for the Privy Seal. I wish all the arrangements of your Government were finally decided, and your great offices efficiently filled. The appearance of hesitation to come forward at this moment has an unfortunate aspect. I am sorry to see, from the public prints, and to hear from other quarters, that Sir James Harris is appointed to the Hague. I did indeed hope that that appointment was destined for my friend Fitzherbert; and, in fact, I thought his pretensions to that embassy were established before I left England. Surely his claims must be superior *with you* to those of Sir James Harris; and certainly no minister who has borne the burden of so important a negotiation as the last peace, and which he managed with so much dexterity and address, was ever worse provided for. I cannot forbear making one more remark on the different arrangements and promotions which have taken place, and expressing concern, that in the course of them Lord Shelburne was not taken some notice of. For office, I put him out of the question; but in the promotion of the peerage he might have been offered a step; and I have reason to believe, that though he has entirely relinquished all views of business and office, yet some mark of distinction, such as that to which I allude, would be peculiarly gratifying to him. The Government (in which my principal object is completed by seeing you placed at the head of it) was first formed under his auspices, and by the quiet manner in which he has quitted his pretensions to any share of it, it certainly owes him some compensation; and except there are reasons with which I am unacquainted, I still hope to see him repaid.

You are so unused to receive letters which contain no application, that, *if it were for form's sake only*, I must recommend one friend, whose interest I have greatly at heart, and who, believe me, will bring no discredit on your patronage and protection. The gentleman I allude to is Captain Molloy, whose name, as a professional man, you cannot be unacquainted with. His finances are very limited, having no other dependence but on the pay of his commission. I urge nothing for him specific or immediate; but in general, if at your leisure you could serve him in any way not incompatible with his profession, either in it or out of it, you would greatly oblige me. I propose, on the first vacancy, to nominate him for one of my boroughs. I must likewise mention to you General Fawcett's views to a red ribbon; at his request I stated them to you in London, and he wishes me to repeat them.

Mr Fox, I am informed, says, " He shall make his harvest from Ireland," but I am persuaded he will find himself deceived. On this country he will not be able to make any impression, nor will it prove in any shape congenial to his views. He seems determined to stop at nothing which may tend to promote his personal success, be the disorders what they may into which his conduct may plunge the country. I trust, however, should he be found transgressing the *exact and proper* limits, that he will not be spared. If he cannot be conciliated or [1]   the country will never be at peace; some stop must be put to a man so turbulent and dangerous, and with so much ability. I am glad the tedious business of the Westminster scrutiny is at last concluded; though the scruples which I find some of your best friends entertained on the proceedings a

[1] The blank thus left in the original.

little alarm me. I hope you have been *strictly correct*, and that the *Westminster scrutiny* may not prove another *Middlesex election*. I have now, my dear Pitt, opened myself to you without the least restraint. I have given you my ideas on a variety of subjects in the most unreserved and familiar manner, not as to a Prime Minister, but to a particular friend. My attachment to you, you must be assured, is the most unequivocal and unalterable; and I am persuaded you have my interests equally at heart, and that your affection for me will be known by its effects. Indeed the confidence which Government has already reposed in me, and the very distinct support which I have received, amply compensates for all the unpleasant circumstances which attend my situation. While my services are acceptable to the King, and while I can promote the mutual interest of both countries, and, at the same time, add any weight to your administration, I shall repent no trouble which may arise, nor wish to relinquish my present office, be the difficulties and dangers ever so great and numerous to which it may be exposed.—Believe me to be, &c.   RUTLAND.

P.S.—My family are all well. I hope Lady Chatham's disorder abates, though I fear but slowly. Give my love to your brother.

THE DUKE OF RUTLAND TO MR PITT.

[*Secret and confidential.*]   DUBLIN CASTLE, *July* 24, 1784.

MY DEAR PITT,—I cannot consistently with my zeal for the King's service, and my affectionate attachment to you, omit transmitting to you as speedily as possible a very flagitious publication which has just been put into my hands, and which will, I suppose, be re-echoed through all the newspapers of this kingdom, and possibly of yours.

Some events have lately occurred which seem to promise consequences worthy of attention, and render it necessary for me to observe upon the facts which I am going to state in order to convey to you an idea of the present situation of things here, and enable you to form such judgment as will tend to decide upon that conduct which I am ready to adopt as best calculated to preserve the quiet and advance the prosperity of the empire.

I have some time entertained suspicions that the lower classes of the people may have been wrought upon by French or American emissaries, from a general endeavour to mix the Roman Catholics with questions of parliamentary reform, and I have therefore on my part endeavoured to detach them as much as possible from mingling in those pursuits. The present season for re-viewing the volunteers has furnished an incident which I am not without hopes will go, not only to weaken the improper influence of those armed bodies, but may possibly lead to their gradual dissolution. Lord Charlemont, the reviewing general of the volunteers, has, in an answer to one of their addresses in the north, given a decided opinion of his disapprobation of admit-ting Roman Catholics to any right of voting, which opinion directly tends to divide the volunteers into two classes, and, of course, to crumble both. I did apprehend Lord Charle-mont's stopping short would push forward the Bishop of Derry,[1] but I could scarcely have conceived that his lordship would have gone so very far as he has done in the enclosed publica-tion, especially as his near connection with Lord Mulgrave on your side of the water, and his brother Mr Phipps, now one of my aide-de-camps here, gave me hopes that he would have con-tented himself with those enormities of which he had been guilty in the administration of Lord Northington, in the face of Parliament.

The question, therefore, is, what is now prudent to be done, for I shall most cheerfully execute whatever shall be thought wisest and best, feeling, as I own I do, much indignation at the daring

[1] Frederick fourth Earl of Bristol, and Bishop of Derry.

and indecent conduct of this extraordinary English peer, and more extraordinary Irish prelate.

But under the impressions of those feelings I ask myself, whether the present, like former seditious publications, may not die away, unless these sparks are kindled by the breath of Government.

Whether these factions which the Duke of Portland's administration has planted in this country may not acquire strength by placing the Bishop of Derry at the head of the Papists and all the malcontents who openly or secretly abet Mr Fox and his adherents here; whether taking any step avowedly against the Bishop at present may not bring on such a general scene of discontent as may lead to invite foreign assistance, and make Ireland, as far as she can, imitate America; and whether anything can be effectually done in this recess of Parliament here, or at all events before the sitting of the courts of justice in November next; though I think any redress to be expected there far inadequate to his lordship's offences:

Whether, again, as an English peer, this intemperate mischievous man may not be more effectually punished or quieted by an English Parliament now sitting, than by any step that can be taken here :

These are considerations which I thought proper to be suggested to you, and perhaps to the Cabinet; in the meantime I have thought it my duty to send to the Attorney and Solicitor General to collect such evidence of these publications as may bring the facts home to the Bishop, which, I understand, was all that had been attempted by my predecessor, and that too without effect; for no evidence of actual writing, or, I believe, of publishing, these seditious addresses, has yet been obtained by all the vigilance of my immediate predecessor, during whose time these seditious publications first made their appearance.

I have not thought it necessary to call any meeting of the Law Servants together upon this subject as yet, nor shall I before I hear from you; and I thought it would be imprudent to call upon any of the principal people of the country until it should become necessary to require their support, which would be premature before the sitting of Parliament, or until some act should be committed which might make it incumbent on me to alarm their fears for the peace of the kingdom in general.

These are the ideas which have struck me as necessary to be communicated to you. Whatever shall be thought wise to do upon them, or if anything more than a general and vigilant attention on my part, your signifying to me either his Majesty's commands or your own wishes will contribute much to my happiness, and I shall instantly take such part as may be deemed most conducive to the general welfare,—I am, &c.,

RUTLAND.

MR PITT TO THE DUKE OF RUTLAND.

DOWNING STREET,
Wednesday, July 28, 1784.

MY DEAR DUKE,—I am extremely obliged to you for your very full and interesting communication. The pressing business of the House of Commons has prevented my being enabled to answer it till this moment. I thought it my duty, from the importance of the subject, to lay your Grace's letter before the King; and I received his Majesty's commands to consult with the Cabinet upon it. With regard to the complexion of the letter which has been printed in Lord Bristol's name, there could be but one opinion. Although the publication (unless it should be coupled with some act in consequence that might be construed into levying war) can hardly be supposed to be treasonable, it is at the same time so daring a libel, and so gross an insult on all government, that it is impossible not to feel the strongest wish to bring the author of it to punishment. But in pursuing the consideration of this subject his Majesty's servants are equally unanimous in thinking that it is involved in considerable difficulty, both with regard to the expediency of proceeding to such measures as the case may seem to call for, and as to the prospect of reaching the principal delinquent, Lord Bristol, with effect. On the latter question, which I will speak of first, as being the simplest, it occurs that the publication, in its present shape, only affords ground of prosecution against the printer, and cannot furnish any ground against Lord Bristol, unless your inquiries succeed to fix upon him the writing or publishing it, or unless the printer, on being proceeded against, should give him up as the author. As to the expediency of any such proceeding, the arguments which your Grace states for consideration have undoubtedly great weight. The notice taken of this offence might, as is often the case, serve to give new popularity and consequence to the offender. In the temper in which some parts of Ireland appear, even the cause of the printer, if he were the object of prosecution, might perhaps be made to raise a cry, however ill-founded, in the country. If the prosecution against him should lead to direct proof against Lord Bristol, there is perhaps still more reason to apprehend that he might avail himself of the present conjuncture, and of the appearance of being persecuted, which is always easily assumed, and always popular, to strengthen his party, particularly by endeavouring to make a common interest with the Roman Catholics.   If the intemperance and delusion of any considerable number should render him successful in that attempt, it might, in the present state of Ireland, lead to consequences which ought not to be hazarded without being fully prepared to meet them.   To all these considerations it must undoubtedly be added, that if, from want of evidence or any other cause, the attempt to punish should prove unsuccessful, it cannot fail to weaken the credit of Government, and give fresh strength and spirit to its opponents.   On every account, therefore, we conclude that no step whatever should be taken against Lord Bristol without the most unequivocal proofs to support them ; and that no step of any sort ought to be taken in relation to the business without most maturely considering, on the best information of the prevailing temper and actual circumstances of the country, what effect may be expected.   The King's servants do not feel themselves sufficiently masters of every consideration that would make a part of this question to form an adequate and decisive opinion at this moment.   They conceive

the less inconvenience is likely to result from
the suspension of any positive determination, as
they apprehend that it is impossible any prosecution can be set on foot before the beginning
of the term; and that therefore that interval
will allow them the opportunity of more fully
considering the subject before it is necessary
that Government should be committed in it.
Your Grace, undoubtedly, has judged very
wisely in ordering measures to be taken immediately to collect evidence; but the reasons
I have before stated make it desirable that they
should be taken privately, without any osten-
sible act on the part of Government. It seems
also, on the same account, proper not to convene
any formal meeting of the Law Servants, or to
take, in any shape, any public notice of this
business, till it is riper than at present.

Any proceeding in this country against Lord
Bristol as a British peer would, in the present
circumstances, be liable to most of the same
objections, and appears besides to involve many
others. I have now troubled your Grace with
all that I am enabled to state to you on this
subject. Though I have on this occasion been
so far from assisting you with a formed and
decisive opinion, I cannot conclude without
assuring you that we are all sensible of the
necessity of forming upon due deliberation

some systematic line of conduct, which, when thoroughly weighed, must be steadily adhered to, as the only chance of extricating the interests of this country in Ireland from the delicate situation in which they are placed, and of preserving the tranquillity of that kingdom. Till such a line of conduct can be fully concerted, I feel that your Grace's task is necessarily, to a certain degree, to temporise, which is never pleasant, and can never for any long time be safe. For every public and private reason, you will not doubt of my sincere wish to relieve you from the necessity of such a conduct, by every exertion which I can contribute to your assistance. —I am ever, my dear Duke, your most faithful and affectionate friend,   W. PITT.

P.S.—This letter is already too long to mix any other subject with it, but I will trouble you on two or three other points of some moment as soon as I can find half an hour.

MR PITT TO THE DUKE OF RUTLAND.

[*Private.*]   PUTNEY HEATH, *Aug.* 9, 1784.

MY DEAR DUKE,—I have been able to write to you much less than I wished, or than I ought. The accumulated business of the session is now drawing to a point, and gives me a prospect of leisure to communicate more fully on the numberless interesting topics which we have to think of during the recess. The immediate object I have in writing at this moment is to state to you some circumstances relative to Lord Mornington, and to beg you to let me know how far the ideas I have conceived on the subject correspond with yours. I find he considers himself as entitled, from the assurances he received both from you and me (either personally or through Lord Temple), before you went to Ireland, to expect the earliest mark of the favour of government in that country which its circumstances could admit of. He expresses a full disposition to have made every allowance for the exigencies of a new government, at so critical a time, but I think he seems to imagine that there was an appearance of his pretensions being postponed, either without sufficient grounds, or without their being so confidentially stated to him as he supposed he had a claim to. He seems at the same time to feel a real zeal for the interests and credit of your government, and a strong sense of the marks of your personal friendship. I am very anxious, for all our sakes, that there should be no misapprehension on the subject, both from a high opinion of him, and from feeling (as I am sure you will) a great desire that

anything like an engagement, or even a reasonable expectation, should not be disappointed.
As far as I recollect what passed, it was in contemplation that new offices would be erected in
the House of Lords, and he had reason to think
that his taking so forward a part would ensure
his being the first to be included in any such
arrangement; or, if that could not be effected,
that he would receive some other mark of the
favour of Government. It seems, I think, not
clear whether such a new arrangement can be
formed; but if it cannot, I think he has a fair
claim to expect the first office that may become
vacant worth his taking, unless he should himself, on all the circumstances being stated to
him, choose to waive it, for the accommodation
of Government. Will you be so good to let me
know whether you agree to this state of the
business.   It is important to have everything
of this nature fully understood, and I am sure
your feelings upon it will be the same as my
own, if you understand it to be as I conceive.

I had a letter by the post to-day from Mr
Orde, the accounts in which I thought very
promising; but I have been very much morti-
fied in learning since that the unlucky adventure
of some frolicsome officers has threatened serious
consequences.   I am very impatient to learn the
particulars, for there seems nothing to be so

much dreaded as any provocation or pretext for the spirit of discontent, which, if no such is afforded, will be ultimately checked by its own excesses, and by the steadiness of Government. I do not know enough of the particulars to form an opinion, but, in writing privately to you, I throw out my first thoughts on the moment. If there is a possibility of your quietly getting rid of the persons concerned in the riot, I think it should be done without loss of time. Government should be kept as distinct as possible from any effects of the indiscretion of individuals, and it seems essential to mark the disavowal as coming from Government voluntarily, and not as a surrender. At all events such a ground of quarrel as this will be a very bad one to be committed upon. I need not tell you that I write this in the utmost haste, nor beg you to consider it as entirely for your own reading. I date from a place I have taken for the summer, next to what was Lord Ashburton's, and which will probably be the farthest point of my excursions from London for most part of the year. We have brought our session nearly to a conclusion, and in the most satisfactory manner for the present, as well as the most promising for the future. But though the pressing business of the day is over, and the immediate contests of party here leave no longer anything formid-

able, the real situation of the country, and its
permanent concerns, leave enough upon our
hands. Your task is not the lightest, and fully
requires all the temper and firmness with which
you have met it. Adieu. Be so good to give
my best respects to the Duchess.—Believe me
ever, my dear Duke, your most faithful and
affectionate friend,　　　　　　　　W. PITT.

THE DUKE OF RUTLAND TO MR PITT.

[*Most private.*]　　　　　PHŒNIX PARK, *August* 15, 1784.

MY DEAR PITT,—You are entitled to my best
thanks for your very candid and satisfactory
letter, which, though it did not exactly apply to
my feelings, yet it removed great doubt and uneasiness from my mind, by pointing out the conduct which I was to adopt in the present critical
moment, and at the same time by giving me
assurances that a fixed and systematic plan
should be determined upon in Cabinet for the
future government of Ireland. The system of
palliations and temporising expedients can never
be conducive to any solid and permanent purpose. A government whose schemes extend no
further than the exigencies of the day cannot
expect any decisive good effects from its measures. Ireland has already been reduced to its

present state of faction and confusion by the not daring to meet and oppose difficult questions in a manly and undaunted manner. You feel for the embarrassments of my situation, and I trust therefore will take early steps to relieve me from them. You may depend upon my not rashly involving your Government; but whenever a fixed and *extended* system shall be recommended, I will pledge myself that it shall be pursued with steadiness and vigour. This city is, in a great measure, under the dominion and tyranny of the mob. Persons are daily marked out for the operation of tarring and feathering; the magistrates neglect their duty, and none of the rioters (till to-day, when one man was seized in the fact) have been taken, while the corps of volunteers in the neighbourhood seem, as it were, to countenance these outrages. In short, the state of Dublin calls loudly for an immediate and vigorous interposition of Government.

In consequence of the letter from Mr Miles to Sir Edward Newenham, which you transmitted to me, I have directed Sir Edward's correspondence to be opened, and I find in the course of it that Mr Miles professes much attachment to you, and wishes to be employed by you as a writer in defence of your Government. His terms appear to be very moderate, as he states that £100 a-year, in addition to his present income, would render him completely contented. He is certainly a writer of abilities, and I think it is worth your while to negotiate with him; but of this you must judge.   I must, however, likewise inform you, that he is a bitter enemy to Lord Temple ; and I think it necessary to send you an extract from the letter, that Lord Temple may be on his guard.   You will perceive, from the manner in which the information is derived, that this is a delicate circumstance.   You will therefore judge how far his lordship is to be depended upon, and how prudent it will be to communicate to him this information.   If you mention it, do it with a civil compliment from me, and render him sensible of the obligation. He states, " that Lord Temple had given a place of £800 per annum to a Mr Doyle, who has only distinguished himself by his profligacy and de- baucheries."   He requests Sir E. to send him the particulars of Mr Doyle's appointment to this office, and he says, " I will then give Lord Tem- ple a letter, every word of which shall go to his soul, and make him tremble.   If my information speaks truth, Lord Temple is a *liar;* he has broke his word with me ; used me cruelly ill ; and by all that is sacred I will publish to the world my whole correspondence with him, in which you (Sir E. Newenham) will appear to a glorious advantage, and his (Lord Temple's) opinion and his character of your Parliament, together with his principles, will damn him in the opinion of all good men." I think my conduct to Lord Temple is very candid and liberal, for I confess I do not believe his lordship to be a sincere friend to my Government. He has laid difficulties in my way, and I must attribute Lord Mornington's present discontent to his suggestions.—I had written thus far when your letter of the 9th arrived. I cannot recollect having made Lord Mornington any specific offer, and indeed he very honourably engaged without terms. How far Lord Temple may have dipped Government by a direct engagement I cannot say; but he was not authorised by me. I can have no hesitation of saying that Lord Mornington shall have the first office which may fall worthy of his acceptance. His merits are very great, which I am sure I am one of the first men to allow. The creation of new offices is a matter for which a congenial moment should be taken. The place to which he particularly turns his eyes is in possession of *a man who is more famous for accumulating office than relinquishing it;* we have already tried him by proposing an arrangement, but as yet he turns a deaf ear to our wishes. Lord Mornington, as I have always stated to him, stands first for whatever may offer. I have his interest much at heart, as well from private regard as from a conviction of his powers to render the public essential service; and the impracticability has been the only obstacle in the way of gratifying his views.

The riot which you allude to has been, as you may imagine, much exaggerated by the prints and by the faction, who wish to create all the mischief possible. It was, however, very unfortunately timed, and an exceedingly foolish drunken business. I was in the country when it happened. At first I determined to dismiss those in my family who were concerned in it; but on reconsideration, as a suit at law was instituted, I thought it more just to forbid the delinquents from appearing in my presence till after their trial, when, if their culpability is strongly proved, I intend to remove them entirely. I likewise directed General Pitt to write a very strong letter of disapprobation to the garrison, and to issue out very peremptory orders respecting officers appearing drunk in the streets, which he did very completely. I hope this line of conduct will seem to you as wise and more candid than hastier measures. The present occurrences of this country you will learn from an office letter which (if not already gone) will go with the messenger who conveys this; and I refer you to a letter which I shall write to Lord Sydney by the same conveyance, where you will find that I have discovered a clue by which I trust I shall find my way to the bottom of all the plots which are contriving in this country. They are entirely French and Roman Catholic, and the leaders of faction in this metropolis are the centre of them. A striking example is wanting, and must be produced, for the benefit of future tranquillity ; and if you will not consent to Lord Bristol's *treasons* being noticed, at least I hope some object equally worthy of punishment may be laid hold of. I have much more to write to you respecting the arrangements here, and points to propose to your consideration, which might serve me, and perhaps be striking to Ireland. I want to sift you respecting the unanimity of your Cabinet, but my paper is exhausted, and I fear I have intruded too much on your time.—So believe me to be the most attached of your friends, RUTLAND.

Excuse blots.

MR PITT TO THE DUKE OF RUTLAND.

[*Private.*]   PUTNEY HEATH, *Oct.* 7, 1784.

MY DEAR DUKE, — I have been intending every day for some time past to trouble you with a letter ; though in many respects I cannot write so fully as the important subjects in question require, till I receive materials of information which I expect from the result of Mr Orde's inquiries, and from the various questions I have persecuted him with. I am in hopes now that your situation is such as to allow a little more respite from the incessant calls of the day, and to furnish leisure for going forward in the great and complicated questions we have to settle before the meeting of Parliament. I have desultorily, at different times, stated in my letters to him the ideas floating in my mind, as the subjects in question carried me to them ; and I have not troubled you with any repetition of them, because I knew you would be acquainted with them as far as they were worth it ; and they certainly were neither distinct nor digested enough to deserve being written twice. I feel, however, notwithstanding the difficulty of deciding upon many of the delicate considerations which present themselves in the arduous business you have in your hands, that a plan must be concerted on all the points, and as far as possible adapted to all the contingencies that may happen, before the meeting of Parliament. The commercial points of discussion, though numerous and comprehensive, may certainly be ascertained and reduced to clear principles by diligent investigation. The internal question of parliamentary reform, though simpler, is perhaps more difficult and hazardous; and the line of future permanent connection between the two countries must be the result of both the preceding questions, and of such arrangements as must accompany a settlement of them. I am revolving these in every shape in my mind; and when I have had the information which I hope to receive in Mr Orde's next packets, I trust I shall be able to send you the best result of my judgment, which I shall wish to submit to your private consideration, in order to learn confidentially the extent of your ideas on the whole plan to be pursued, before it is formally brought under the consideration of the Cabinet here.

I own to you the line to which my mind at present inclines (open to whatever new observations or arguments may be suggested to me) is, *to give Ireland an almost unlimited communication of commercial advantages*, if we can receive in return some security that *her strength and riches will be our benefit, and that she will contribute from time to time in their increasing proportions to the common exigencies of the empire.* And having, by holding out this, removed, I trust, every temptation to Ireland to consider her interest as separate from England, to be ready, while we discountenance *wild and unconstitutional attempts, which strike at the root of all authority,* to give real efficacy and popularity to Government, by acceding (if such a line can be found) to a *prudent and temperate reform of Parliament*, which may guard against or gradually cure *real* defects and mischiefs, may show a sufficient regard to the interests and even prejudices of individuals who are concerned, and may unite the Protestant interest in *excluding the Catholics from any share in the representation* or the government of the country.

The propriety and practicability of this, as of everything else, must depend upon the actual temper and disposition of men's minds, and upon a full view of all relative circumstances, more, perhaps, than upon the abstract consideration of the thing itself. As such I do not state my opinion as finally formed, but I am anxious to state to you the present inclination of my mind, and to learn yours in return. You, who have the great task of executing any plan, are in a situation to suggest innumerable observations which my view of the subject cannot furnish me with. The sooner, upon full communication, we can ultimately decide, and set on foot all the operations with regard to the instruments and the detail by which any plan of one sort or other is to be effected, the better. In the interval, there seems no one *immediately* pressing

object but the *approaching congress*, if indeed
the congress is to meet, which, after what has
passed, I think doubtful. That it should not
meet, or that it should meet in a shape to defeat itself (without any other intervention), is
the great object to be wished. But it is of the
utmost importance *what line you adopt in case
of its meeting*. Perhaps *the leaving it* to itself
is, all things considered, the wisest. At all
events it seems to me *essential* not by any means
to pledge Government on that occasion against
the *possibility of adopting any reform, however
modified.* But on this particular point of the
congress I am in hopes we shall, by the next
messenger, receive a full account of your ideas
of what is to be done, as well as of what has
passed, on the subject of reform in the different
counties. Let me beseech you at all events to
let us hear from you fully on this matter, time
enough to return an answer before their assem-
bling, as any step taken in relation to it may lead
to important consequences. It is principally
with this view that I trouble you with this
messenger, which I should not have thought
necessary till I could have given you the result
of more consideration, if this period had not
been so near.—Adieu for the present, and believe me ever, my dear Duke, most faithfully
and affectionately yours,   W. PITT.

MR PITT TO THE DUKE OF RUTLAND.

DOWNING STREET, *Oct.* 7, [1784.]

MY DEAR DUKE,—In reflecting on my way to town on the subject of the letter which accompanies this, there occurs to me one material circumstance, which, as I wish not to withhold from you any thought that occurs to me, makes me add this short postscript. I have stated that the propriety or practicability of any plan of reform must be tried in a great measure by the temper of the people. I see how great the difficulty of your situation must be in this respect, because it must have naturally happened that the persons with whom you have necessarily most habits of intercourse must be those who are most interested against any plan of reform; that is to say, those who have the greatest share of present parliamentary interest. What I venture to suggest for your consideration is, whether it be possible for you to gain any authentic knowledge (without committing yourself) of the extent of the numbers who are really zealous for reform, and of the ideas that would content them. By all I hear accidentally, the Protestant reformers are alarmed at the pretensions of the Catholics, and for that very reason would stop very short of the extreme speculative notions of universal suffrage. Could there be any way of your confidentially sounding Lord Charlemont, without any danger from the consequences? I am sure you will forgive the anxiety which impels me to trouble you with all these suggestions. I am aware you may have seen local difficulties which may discourage you in this whole subject of reform, and make you doubt the possibility of applying our principles to Ireland; but let me beseech you to recollect, that both your character and mine for consistency are at stake, unless there are unanswerable proofs that the case of Ireland and England is different; and to recollect also, that however it is our duty to oppose the most determined spirit and firmness to ill-grounded clamour or factious pretensions, it is a duty equally indispensable to take care not to struggle but in a *right cause.* Adieu. I will not allow myself to trouble you any more at present.—Ever yours, W. PITT.

THE DUKE OF RUTLAND TO MR PITT.

PHŒNIX PARK, *Nov.* 4, 1784.

MY DEAR PITT,—Lord Mornington has suggested an idea, and he has desired me to state it to you, by which our mutual wishes to gratify him in his objects may be accomplished in their fullest extent. In the event of Lord Walsingham's appointment to India, which I understand is intended, a Vice-Treasurership of Ireland will become vacant. Would it be inconsistent with any rules which may be laid down by Administration in England to appoint him as the successor to that office ? We both, I am convinced, feel anxious on every account to see Lord Mornington placed in a situation where he may be pledged as an avowed and responsible [member] of Government in both countries, and if this arrangement could be made in his favour, all difficulties respecting him would be removed. I confess I cannot but be extremely anxious to see his views gratified, both from the high opinion I have formed of his abilities and merits, as well as from the real and sincere regard I bear him personally, and in both of which I am satisfied you are not behindhand with me.—I am, &c.,   RUTLAND.

MR PITT TO THE DUKE OF RUTLAND.

[*Private.*]   DOWNING STREET,
                                 Thursday Night, Nov. 4, 1784.

MY DEAR DUKE,—I find a messenger is just setting out; I have therefore time at present only for a few very hasty lines. I congratulate you on all the fruits of your perseverance, which

I trust are improving every day. Much, however, yet remains to be settled. The more I proceed in the investigation of the commercial points, the more confirmed I am in hoping that there is no difficulty there which may not be surmounted, if Ireland can be brought to repay, as she ought, the concession of full *equality in commerce* by a very *moderate contribution* to our burdens, particularly to our sinking fund. I am extremely anxious to hear from you on the subject of the long letter I troubled you with some time since, for be assured *our character, our credit, and our success is deeply involved in the issue of that business.* The next great object is that of the measures to be taken *with respect to the volunteers.* The converting them into militia (which you point at in your last letter to Lord Sydney), or the bringing them some way or other under the sanction and control of the executive Government, cannot be kept too constantly in view. The great difficulty I see in the idea of a militia arises from the large proportion of Catholics, which might make it hardly possible, in some counties, to find means for a Protestant corps. I wish you would have the detail of any ideas you have formed on this subject, with the difficulties, and the means of solving them, thrown into shape as soon as may be. I will trouble you or Mr Orde with whatever presents itself to me on this capital object from time to time. My great wish is, that all the several leading points may be enough digested to be considered *in one view, and as members of one general system,* to be decided on by the Cabinet long before the Parliament of either country meets; and I wish to communicate most fully with you before anything is formally and ministerially proposed. Adieu.— Ever most affectionately and faithfully yours,

W. Pitt.

I will write to you very soon on the private subjects in your last letter, on which I need not say I will do whatever I can.

MR PITT TO THE DUKE OF RUTLAND.

[*Most private.*] Putney Heath, *Dec.* 4, 1784.

My dear Duke,—I am happy to tell you that our commercial arrangements have appeared more easy and unexceptionable, the more we have talked them over. A system of the utmost liberality and of perfect equality (with only some exceptions *in favour of Ireland*) is, I think, not difficult to be adjusted, if the principle on which it can alone be justified can be carried throughout. The great point on which

I find Foster and Beresford, and even Orde, entertain a doubt, is the stipulating some contribution in return from Ireland. I perceive by your last letter you see the objections in the same light as they do; but I really believe those objections may be removed; and I do not see *the possibility* of agreeing to complete the system of *equal commerce* (which is what must be now done) without some *return* being *secured* to this country. The return ought to be proportioned, not merely to what we have now to give (which, however, in the estimation of Ireland itself, is considerable), but to all that has been given since the first concessions from the year 1778 downwards. The manner in which those concessions were unhappily made precluded any return, either in direct compensation, or even, to any great degree, in general zeal and gratitude. But now the *balance is to be struck* and the *account closed* between the two countries, and we must *take full credit*, as well for what has been given (however improvidently in the mode of doing it) by others, as for whatever we may be [able] to give ourselves. I am ready, at the same time, to admit, that the equivalent due from Ireland is not to be expected *immediately*. Give us only a *certainty* that if your extended commerce increases your revenue, the surplus, after defraying the same proportion of Irish

expenses as at present, shall go to relieve us.
This, I think, no Irishman can rationally object
to, and Englishmen will be satisfied, though at
present the equivalent will certainly be below
the just proportion.   Your idea respecting the
militia, &c., deserves every attention, from the
importance of the object on the one hand, and
the difficulty of execution on the other.   Parliamentary reform, I am still sure, after considering all you have stated, *must* sooner or later be
carried in *both countries*.   If it is well done, the
sooner the better.   I will write to you, by as
early an opportunity as I can, the full result of
all my reflections on the subject.   For God's
sake, do not persuade yourself, in the meantime, that the measure, if properly managed,
and separated *from every ingredient of faction*
(which I believe it may be), is inconsistent with
either the dignity or the tranquillity and facility
of Government.   On the contrary, I believe *they*
ultimately depend upon it.   And if such a settlement is practicable, it is the only system worth
the hazard and trouble which belongs to every
system that can be thought of.   I write in great
haste, and under a strong impression of these
sentiments.   You will perceive that this is
merely a confidential and personal communication between you and myself, and therefore I
need add no apology for stating so plainly

what is floating in my mind on these subjects.—
Believe me ever, my dear Duke, most faithfully
and affectionately yours, W. PITT.

MR PITT TO THE DUKE OF RUTLAND.

[*Most private.*] PUTNEY HEATH, *Dec.* 14, 1784.

MY DEAR DUKE,—I cannot easily express to
you the anxiety we have felt here from the
account of your illness, and the proportionate
pleasure we feel in learning the progress of your
recovery. I hope and trust, for all our sakes,
you will do yourself justice, and not be too
impatient to be well. If anything could add
to my personal interest in your health from
affection and attachment, it would be the actual
situation of affairs at this moment. We have
everything to hope from a permanent settlement in the approaching session, if vigilance,
temper, and firmness can ensure its success. But
the stake is a deep one, and much depends upon
it. I will not detain you now by writing at
length. I enclose a letter of ten days ago,
which I was then prevented from sending by
the cruel alarm of your illness. On the commercial points we have scarcely any longer any
difficulty, if *some mode* and *time* of contribution
(accommodated in any manner to the temper of

Ireland) can be fixed. Without this, the difficulty is infinite; and there is nothing I will not
submit to sooner than to bring forward a lame
and imperfect system, adding to concessions on
the one hand, without affording a reasonably
secure expectation of return on the other.
With regard to parliamentary reform, it requires every sort of management in the mode
and the conduct of it; but the substance of it
cannot be finally resisted, either with prudence
or with credit. I am ashamed of crowding so
much business into a letter the first object of
which was to carry you the affectionate congratulations of a cordial friend, which do not
deserve to be named with politics; but as the
session is approaching, the time presses. I hope
you have the prospect of recovering strength
fast enough to meet the trials of your situation
in this decisive moment, with the same exertion
and success which has happily thus far rewarded
your labours. You are sure in every situation,
and in every possible event, of my warmest and
most anxious wishes, both as a public and a
private man. I must not conclude without
telling you that we look forward to our parliamentary campaign with every prospect of
abundant security, and, what is much better, of
the means of improving essentially the situation
and credit of the country. You will have re-

ceived long since the account of our Marquesses [1] and of Lord Camden,[2] which I am sure you will have approved. — Ever, my dear Duke, most sincerely and affectionately yours,

W. PITT.

MR PITT TO THE DUKE OF RUTLAND.

[*Secret.*]   DOWNING STREET, *Jan.* 6, 1785.

MY DEAR DUKE,—You will receive by the messenger from Lord Sydney the official com- munication of the unanimous opinion of the Cabinet on the subject of the important settle- ment to be proposed as final and conclusive be- tween Great Britain and Ireland. The objects have been considered with all possible atten- tion; and though minuter inquiry may still be necessary with regard to some few points in- cluded in the propositions, we are so fully satis- fied with the general principles on which they rest that they are without hesitation transmitted to your Grace, as containing the substance of a system from which it appears wholly impossible for us to depart. I am confirmed by the opinion of Mr Foster and Mr Beresford, as well as Mr

---

[1] The Earl of Shelburne was created Marquess of Lansdowne, and the Earl Temple Marquess of Buckingham.

[2] Lord Camden was promoted to an earldom, May 13, 1786. There was probably an earlier promise, to which Mr Pitt refers.

Orde, that the complete liberty and equality in matters of trade which will by this plan be given to Ireland ought to give the fullest satisfaction on that subject; and if that opinion is enforced, and supported by all the arguments it admits, and vigorous exertions used to circulate it, I trust your Grace will meet with less difficulty than has been imagined in obtaining from Ireland those measures on their part which are indispensable to accompany it, in order to make the advantage reciprocal, and of course to make the system either consistent or durable. I am not sanguine enough to suppose that any plan could at once be accepted with universal approbation.   No great settlement of this extent was ever carried without meeting some, perhaps strong, objections, and without requiring much management and perseverance to accomplish it; but they will, I am sure, not be wanting on your part; and considering the strength of Government in Parliament, and all the circumstances of the country, it is impossible to believe that your friends and supporters should have really any hesitation, if they once understand, what they must know sooner or later, that the settlement between the two kingdoms, and of course the giving tranquillity to Ireland, and security to any interest *they* have at stake, must turn on this fundamental and

essential point, *of reciprocity in the final compact to be now formed.* If the point is secured
in Parliament, *which I cannot allow myself to
doubt,* I do not apprehend much additional
clamour or discontent without doors. It will
be difficult for malice and faction to find many
topics calculated to catch the mind of the public,
if the nature of the measure is fairly stated, and
sufficiently explained in its true light. I am
unwilling to trouble you at present very much
at length, and have myself little time to spare;
but yet I have the success of this whole arrangement so much at heart, from every personal and
public feeling, knowing that your credit and my
own are equally concerned with the interest of
both countries, and the future prosperity of the
empire, that you will, I am sure, forgive me, if
I call your attention more particularly to what
strikes me as the true state of *what* it is which
we propose to give, and *what* we require in return. If it appears to you in the same light as
it does to me, I trust you will feel the impossibility of our reconciling our minds to waive so
essential an object. I assure you there is scarce
a man whom I have here consulted who does not
feel it at least as strongly as I do. The general
tenor of our propositions not only gives a full
equality to Ireland, but extends that principle
to many points where it would be easy to have

urged just exceptions, and in many other points possibly turns the scale in her favour, at a risk, perhaps a remote one, of considerable local disadvantages to many great interests of this country. I do not say that in practice I apprehend the effect on our trade and manufactures will be such as it will perhaps be industriously represented; but I am persuaded (whatever may be the event) that by the additions now proposed to former concessions we open to Ireland the chance of a competition with ourselves, on terms of more than equality, and we give her advantages which make it impossible she should ever have anything to fear from the jealousy or restrictive policy of this country in future. Such an arrangement is defensible only on the idea of relinquishing local prejudices and partial advantages, in order to consult uniformly and without distinction the general benefit of the empire. This cannot be done but by making England and Ireland *one country* in effect, though for local concerns under distinct Legislatures; *one* in the communication of advantages, and of course in the participation of burdens. If their *unity* is broken, or rendered absolutely *precarious*, in either of these points, the system is defective, and there is an end of the whole. The two capital points are, the construction of the Navigation Act, and the system of duties on the importation into either country of the manufactures of the other. With regard to the Navigation Act, it has been claimed by the advocates for Ireland as a matter of justice, on the ground that the same Act of Parliament must bear the same construction in its operation on Ireland as on Great Britain. Even on the narrow ground of *mere construction*, it may well be argued as at *least doubtful* whether the provisoes in the Act of 14th and 15th C. II. (by which it was in effect adopted by authority of the Irish Parliament) do not plainly do away that restriction on imports of colony produce from England to Ireland which is not done away by any proviso or otherwise with regard to the same importation from Ireland into England. On such a supposition it might be very consistent that the Act of Navigation should be enforced here (as it was by subsequent Acts of Parliament) in its original strictness, and in Ireland with those exceptions in favour of colony produce imported from hence which the provisoes I allude to seem to have admitted; and the practice of more than a hundred years has been conformable to this distinction. But this is on the mere *point of* construction. The question is, not merely what has been or ought to be the construction of the existing law, but what is really fair in the relative situation of the

two countries. Here, I think, it is universally
allowed, that, however just the claim of Ireland
is not to have her own trade *fettered and re-
stricted*, she can have no claim to any share
beyond what we please to give her in the trade
of our colonies. They belong (unless by favour
or by compact we make it otherwise) *exclusively
to this country*. The suffering Ireland to send
anything to those colonies, to bring anything
directly from thence, is itself *a favour*, and is a
deviation, too, for the sake of favour to Ireland,
from the general and almost uniform policy of
all nations with regard to the trade of their
colonies. But the present claim of Ireland has
gone further; it is not merely to carry produce
thither, or to bring it from thence, but it is to
supply us, *through Ireland*, with the produce of
our own colonies, in prejudice, as far as it goes,
of the direct trade between those colonies and
this country. Can it be said that Ireland has
any right to have the liberty of thus *carrying
for us*, because we have the liberty of carrying
for them, unless the colonies with whom the
trade subsists are as much *their* colonies as they
are *ours?* It may be true that the favour
granted by former concessions in this respect is
in some measure compensated by their securing
in favour of our colonies a monopoly of their
consumption; though it may well be doubted

whether on any possible supposition they could
be supplied from the colonies of any other country on terms of similar indulgence. But the
liberty to be now given stands on a separate
ground, and is a *mere and absolute favour*, if
ever there was anything that could be called
so. It is a sacrifice, too, which cannot fail to be
magnified here, even beyond its true value, as a
departure from the principles of the Act of Navigation, which has been so long idolised in this
country. But what I principally state this for
is to prove the *liberal and conciliating spirit*
which induces us to agree to the proposal. I do
not wish to exaggerate its probable effects. I
do not expect that in practice it will materially
interfere with the trade of this country; but it
is unquestionably true, that even though we
should not immediately lose by it, yet Ireland
will be considerably benefited, by opening so
near a market, which will encourage her merchants to a freer speculation, and enable them
to avail themselves more than they have hitherto
done of the advantages they are already possessed of. Some persons here may perhaps even
apprehend that the liberty of supplying our
market may *gradually* enable them to lay in
a stock for the supply of other markets also,
which perhaps they could not do otherwise; and
if that should be the effect, not only they will

be gainers, but we shall be losers in the same proportion. On the whole, however, I am fully reconciled to the measure, because even supposing it not to produce these effects it must be remembered that it is a liberty which Ireland has strongly solicited, and on which she *appears to set a high value.* As such, it is the strongest proof of cordiality to grant it, in spite of prevailing and perhaps formidable prejudices; and in truth it establishes in favour of Ireland so intimate a connection and so equal a *participation* with this country, even in those points where we have the fullest right to exclusive advantage, that it gives them an interest in the protection of our colonies and the support of our trade equal in proportion to our own.   I come now to the system of duties between the two countries; and here, too, I think Ireland has not less reason to be satisfied and to be grateful. By lowering our duties to the standard of Ireland we put her in possession of absolute equality, on the face of the arrangement; but I think in truth we put her in possession of something more.   If, however, it were bare equality, we are departing, in order to effect it, from the policy of prohibiting duties so long established in this country.   In doing so we are perhaps to encounter the prejudices of our manufacturing [interests] in every corner of the kingdom.   We are admitting to this competition a country whose labour is cheap, and whose resources are unexhausted; ourselves burdened with accumulated taxes, which are felt in the price of every necessary of life, and of course enter into the cost of every article of manufacture. It is indeed stated on the other hand, that Ireland has neither the skill, the industry, nor the capital of this country; but it is difficult to assign any good reason why she should not gradually, with such strong encouragement, imitate and rival us in both the former, and in both more rapidly from time as she grows possessed of a larger capital, which, with all the temptations for it, may perhaps to some degree be transferred to her from hence, but which will at all events be increased if her commerce receives any extension, and will as it increases necessarily extend that commerce still farther. But there is another important consideration which makes the system of duties more favourable to Ireland than she could expect on the ground of perfect equality. It is this: although the duties taken separately on the importation of each article will be the same in the two countries, it is to be remembered, that there are some articles which may pass from one to the other perfectly free; consequently, if the articles which in the actual state of the trade we are able to send to Ireland

are those which pay *some* duty, if the articles
which she principally sends to us are articles
which *pay no duty*, can anything be plainer
than that, although upon each article taken
separately there is an appearance of impartial-
ity and equality, the result of the whole is mani-
festly to a great degree *more favourable to Ireland than to this country?*

The case I have just stated will actually exist
with regard to the woollen and linen trades. We
send you a considerable quantity of woollen, *subject to some duty;* you send us linen to an immense amount, *subject to none.* This single circumstance of the linen would have been a fair
and full answer (even without any reduction of
duties on the import of other articles) to the
clamour for protecting duties. The whole
amount of the British manufacture which Ireland
actually takes from England, under *a low duty*,
and on which she has threatened prohibitory
duties, does not amount to so much as the single
article of linen, which we are content to take
from you, *under no duty at all.* I have stated
all this, to show that this part of the arrangement is in the same spirit with the other. What
is it then that can reconcile this country to such
concessions, under these circumstances? It is
perhaps true, that with regard to some of the
articles of manufacture there are particular con-

siderations which make the danger to us less than it might be imagined. In the great article of the woollen, if we confine the raw material to ourselves, and let Ireland do the same, perhaps the produce of Ireland, and what she can import from other places, can never enable her to supplant us to a great extent in this article. This undoubtedly must be our policy, and it makes part of the resolutions proposed; it can never, in my opinion, be thought any exception to the general freedom of trade, nor do I believe any man could seriously entertain any expectation of the contrary line being adopted. If each country is at liberty to make the most of its own natural advantages, it could not be supposed that we should part with a material indispensable to our staple manufacture. If there is any other similar prohibition on the export of raw material now in force in Ireland, it would be equally fair that it should be continued; but, on the other hand, it is essential that no new one should be hereafter imposed in either country, as this part of the system should, like the rest, be finally settled, and not left open to future discussion. But this consideration affects only the particular article of woollen. The fundamental principle, and the only one on which the whole plan can be justified, is, that I mentioned in the beginning of my letter,—that for the future the two countries

E

will be to the most essential purposes united.
On this ground, the wealth and prosperity of the
whole is the object; from what local sources they
arise is indifferent.   We trust to various circumstances, in believing that no branch of trade or
manufacture will shift so suddenly as not to allow
time, in every instance as it arises, for the industry of this country gradually to take another
direction; and confident that there will be markets sufficient to exercise the industry of both
countries, to whatever pitch either can carry it,
we are not afraid in this liberal view to encourage
a competition which will ultimately prove for the
common benefit of the empire, by giving to each
country the possession of whatever branch of
trade or article of manufacture it is best adapted
to, and therefore likely to carry on with the most
advantage.   These are the ideas I entertain of
what we give to Ireland, and of the principles
on which it is given.   The unavoidable consequence of these principles brings me back to that
which I set out with,—the indispensable necessity of some fixed mode of contribution on the
part of Ireland, in proportion to her growing
means, to the general defence.   That in fact she
ought to contribute in that proportion I have
never heard any man question as a principle.
Indeed, without that expectation the conduct of
this country would be an example of rashness

and folly not to be paralleled. But we are desired to content ourselves with the strongest
general pledge that can be obtained of the intention of Ireland, without requiring anything
specific at present. I must fairly say that such
a measure neither can nor ought to give satisfaction. In the first place, it is making everything
take place immediately on our part, and leaving
everything uncertain on that of Ireland, which
would render the whole system so lame and imperfect as to be totally indefeasible. It would
reserve this essential point as a perpetual source
of jealous discussion, and that even in time of
peace, when, with no objects to encourage exertion, men will be much more disposed to object
than to give liberally; and we should have nothing but a vague and perhaps a fallacious hope,
in answer to the clamours and apprehensions of
all the descriptions of men who lose, or think
they lose, by the arrangement. If it is indispensable, therefore, that the contribution should be
in some degree ascertained at present, it is equally
clear, on the other hand, that the quantum of it
must not be fixed to any stated sum, which of
necessity would either be too great at present,
or in a little time hence too small. The only
thing that seems reasonable is to appropriate a
certain fund towards supporting the general expenses of the empire in time of peace, and leave

it, as it must be left, to the zeal of Ireland to provide for extraordinary emergencies in time of war as they arise. The fund which seems the best, and indeed the only one that has been pointed out for this purpose, is the hereditary revenue. Though the effect will not be immediate, our object will be attained if the future surplus of this revenue beyond its present produce, estimated at the medium of the four or five last years, is applied in the manner we wish. Such a fund, from the nature of the articles of which it is composed, must have a direct relation to the wealth, the commerce, and the population of Ireland. It will increase with their extension, and cannot even begin to exist without it. Towards this country it will be more acceptable than a much larger contribution in any other way; because, if in fact the commerce of Ireland should be increased at our expense by our manufactures and trade being transferred in any degree thither, the compensation will arise in the same proportion. It has this further inestimable advantage, from being fixed according to a standard which will apply to all the future circumstances of the two countries, that it will, from the very permanence of the principle, tend to unite them more closely and firmly to each other. In Ireland, it cannot escape consideration, that this is a contribution not given beforehand for uncertain expectations, but which can only follow the actual possession and enjoyment of the benefits in return for which it is given. If Ireland does not grow richer and more populous, she will by this scheme contribute nothing. If she does grow richer by the participation of our trade, surely she ought to contribute, and the measure of that contribution cannot, with equal justice, be fixed in any other proportion. It can never be contended that the increase of the hereditary revenue ought to be left to Ireland as the means of gradually diminishing her other taxes, unless it can be argued that the whole of what Ireland now pays is a greater burden in proportion than the whole of what is paid by this country, and that, therefore, she ought, even if she grows richer, rather to diminish that burden on herself than give anything towards lightening ours. Indeed, if this were argued, it would be an argument, not against this particular mode of contributing, but against any contribution at all. For if Ireland were to contribute voluntarily from time to time, at the discretion of her Parliament, it would, if the contribution were real and effectual, equally prevent any diminution of her own burdens, only the mode and the proportion would be neither so certain nor so satisfactory. It is to be remembered that the very increase supposed to arise in the hereditary revenue cannot arise without a

similar increase in many articles of the additional
taxes; consequently, from that circumstance
alone, though they part with the future increase
of their hereditary revenue, their income will be
upon the whole increased, without imposing any
additional burdens. On the whole, therefore, if
Ireland allows that she ought ever in time of
peace to contribute at all, on which it is impossible to frame a doubt, I can conceive no plausible
objection to the particular mode proposed. I
recollect but two or three topics that have been
suggested as likely to be urged by those who
wish to create difficulties. The first, if it applies
at all, applies as an argument against any contribution of any sort. It is, *that the wealth of Ireland is brought by absentees to be spent in this
country.* In the first place, the amount of this
is indefinite, and the idea, I believe, greatly over-
rated. What this country gains by it I am sure
is small. The way in which it must be supposed
to injure Ireland is, by diminishing the capital
in the country, and by obstructing civilisation
and improvement. If this is true, what follows?
That the effect of this, as far as it operates, to
prevent the increase of trade and riches, will prevent also the existence or the increase of the
fund on which the contribution is to depend.
Therefore this argument, giving it its utmost
weight, does not affect the particular plan in

question. Besides this, Ireland in its present state bears this evil, and under these circumstances supports her present burden. If she grows richer, will she not be able to support, out of that additional wealth, some addition of burden, at least, without any increase of hardship or difficulty? But if Ireland states the wealth we are supposed to draw from her by absentees, on one hand, we may state what she draws from us by commerce on the other. Look at the trade between Great Britain and Ireland, and see how large a proportion of what we take from her is the produce of her soil or the manufactures of her inhabitants (which are the great sources of national riches). How small, comparatively, the proportion of similar articles which she takes from us. The consequence is obvious, that she is, in this respect, clearly more benefited than we are by the intercourse between us.

The other topic is, that it is impolitic and odious that this arrangement should have the appearance of *a bargain*, and such an idea will render it unpopular with the public. If a permanent system is to be settled by the authority of two distinct Legislatures, I do not know what there is more odious in a bargain between them than in a treaty between two separate Crowns. If the bargain is unfair, if the terms of it are not for mutual benefit, it is not calculated for the

situation of two countries connected as Great
Britain and Ireland ought to be. But it is of
the essence of such a settlement (whatever name
is to be given to it) that both *the advantage* and
the obligation should be reciprocal; one cannot
be so without the other. This reciprocity,
whether it is or is not to be called a bargain,
is an inherent and necessary part of the new
system to be established between the two countries. In the relation of Great Britain [with
Ireland] there can subsist but two possible principles of connection. The one, that which is
exploded, of total subordination in Ireland, and
of restrictions on her commerce for the benefit of
this country, which was by this means enabled
to bear the whole burden of the empire; the
other is, what is now proposed to be confirmed
and completed, that of an equal participation of
all commercial advantages, and some proportion
of the charge of protecting the general interest.
If Ireland is at all connected with this country,
and to remain a member of the empire, she must
make her option between these two principles,
and she has wisely and justly made it for the
latter. But if she does think this system for her
advantage as well as ours, and if she sets any
value either on the confirmation and security of
what has been given her, or on the possession of
what is now within her reach, she can attain

neither without performing on her part what both reason and justice entitle us to expect. The only remaining consideration is, for what service this contribution shall be granted, and in what manner it shall be applied. This seems a question of little difficulty. The great advantage that Ireland will derive is, from the equal participation of our trade, and of the benefits derived from our colonies. Nothing, therefore, is so natural, as that she should contribute to the support of the navy, on which the protection of both depends. For the rest, it seems only necessary to provide some proper mode of ascertaining to the Parliament of Ireland, that the surplus is annually paid over, to be applied together with other monies voted here for naval services, and to be accounted for, together with them, to the Parliament of this country. There can be but *one navy* for the empire at large, and it must be administered by the executive power in this country. The particulars of the administration of it cannot be under the control of anything but the Parliament of this country. This principle, on the fullest consideration, seems one which must be held sacred. Nothing else can also prevent the supreme executive power, and with it the force of the empire, being distracted into different channels, and its energy and effect being consequently lost. As the sum to be

received in this manner from Ireland can never
be more than a part (I fear a small one) of the
whole naval expense, as its amount from time to
time will be notorious, and as it will go in diminution of the supplies to be granted here, the
Parliament of this country will have both the
means and the inducement to watch its expendi-
ture as narrowly as if it was granted by themselves.   Ireland, therefore, will have the same
security that we have against any misapplication,
and she will have the less reason to be jealous
on the subject, because we have a common interest with her, and to a still greater extent, in
the service which it is intended to support; and
if any deficiency arises from mismanagement it
will (according to this arrangement) fall, not
upon them, but upon us, to make it good.   I
have no more to add.   I have troubled you with
all this from an extreme anxiety to put you in
possession of all that occurs to me on one of the
most interesting subjects that can occupy our
attention in the course of our lives.   You will,
I am sure, forgive my wearying you with so
much detail.   I release you from it, in the persuasion that you will feel how much depends
upon this crisis for both countries, and in the
certainty that your exertions, and those of your
friends, will be proportioned to its importance.
I will only add, that difficulties may be started

at first, but I think they must vanish on discussion. At all events, believe me, my dear
Duke, it is indispensable to us all, and to the
public, that they should be overcome. By
address and dexterity in the management of the
business, and above all, by firmness and a resolution to succeed, I have no doubt that it will be
found both possible and easy. I shall then have
to congratulate you on your having the happiness to accomplish a scheme which may lay
the foundation of lasting tranquillity and reviving
prosperity to both countries.—I am ever, with
constant affection and attachment, my dear Duke,
your faithful and sincere friend, W. PITT.

DOWNING STREET, *Friday, Jan.* 7, 1785,
½ *past* 12 P.M.

I need hardly tell you that I am obliged to
send you these sheets as they are, without the
leisure either to copy or revise them.

MR PITT TO THE DUKE OF RUTLAND.

[*Most private.*] DOWNING STREET, *Jan.* 11, 1785.

MY DEAR DUKE,—Since I wrote to you last
the Cabinet have again had under consideration
the leading objects which are likely to require
attention in Ireland in the approaching session.

The two great questions, in addition to the commercial arrangement and the mode of contribution (on which I troubled you so much at length
when I wrote last), are those of the reform of
Parliament, and the substitution of a militia in
place of the volunteer army.   On the point of
reform, you will receive from Lord Sydney the
communication of our sentiments, and I trust
you will agree that, under all the circumstances,
the line which has been approved of here is the
only one which can properly be pursued at present.   I am more and more convinced in my
own mind every day some reform will take place
in both countries.   Whatever is to be wished
(on which, notwithstanding numerous difficulties,
I have myself no doubt), it is, I believe, at least
certain, that if any reform takes place here the
tide will be too strong to be withstood in Ire
land.   It seems, therefore, the part of common
prudence to bear in mind that that event is at
least possible, and perhaps not distant, and to
be prepared for the circumstances which it may
produce.   You will, I am sure, feel, that if any
reform is to be brought forward in Ireland with
a probability of success, it is very material to
the interest of that country, as well as to its
connection with this, that Government should
know beforehand the extent in which it is most
likely to be pushed.   It may then be in our

power both to guard against dangerous excesses, and to reconcile, as far as possible, the prejudices and interests of those friends to Government who may be adverse to the measure. I do not speak of this as an easy task, but it will, I am sure, in the contingency I have mentioned, be a necessary one. I think, too, it will not prove impossible, and the taking timely precautions is the way to make it less. There is nothing more dangerous, as it seems to me, than to take for granted that nothing moderate or reasonable can content the friends or be agreed to by the opposers of reform. A prudent Government may, by proper management, go a great way to reconcile extremes. Many of the reformers seem already, from the fear of the Catholics, to be averse to going excessive lengths; and if moderate and peaceable men can be brought to take the lead of the wild and factious incendiaries who have intruded themselves into the management of this business, I cannot think it would be impossible (when the circumstances are ripe for such a measure) to make them sensible that a *temperate* plan may answer every real purpose of security to the constitution. On the other hand, if wild excesses are guarded against, it may surely be practicable (on the supposition of the question having been carried here, to which alone this part of my reasoning is meant to

apply) to satisfy the friends of Government that
the opposition to a moderate plan would be
dangerous and ineffectual.   It will remain to be
seen how far even the interests of those immediately affected by a reform may be considered or
affected; but at all events, if they see it become necessary for the tranquillity of the country
that something should be done, they will have
no ground of complaint against Government.
Indeed, it seems to me that the principal supporters are so strongly bound to stand by it, in
the case I mention, from the deep stake they
have in the country, that there will be no danger,
at any rate, of their taking a part to promote
confusion and disorder.   They are, besides, most
of them, in possession of great present advantages, and look to future objects from the continuance of their attachment, which they will
not lightly abandon.   Much of these considerations, I am aware, is premature; the only inference I draw from them at present is, that it will
be desirable to procure every possible information with regard to the temper of the friends to
a reform, and what moderate men there are
among them, who may, at a proper time, have
weight enough to influence the conduct of the
rest; and also to find out, if possible, how the
prejudices and objections of the enemies to it
may be best surmounted, if the contingency I

have alluded to takes place. When I say this is desirable, I am sensible, at the same time, that it is delicate and difficult to take any step towards it at present; because there is a third consideration, just in the present moment more important than any; I mean that of not shocking or startling any of the friends to Government while the great commercial arrangement is in agitation. For this reason the Cabinet were clearly of opinion, as I found Mr Orde was, and I have no doubt you will be, that it was advisable at all events to postpone discussing the question of reform till it has been decided here; and in the meantime it is certainly not the business of Government *to pledge itself to anything.* It would be unfair to make the friends of Government believe that any reform is at all events to be opposed; it would be unreasonable and imprudent to let them suppose it is at all events to be supported, which cannot be decided till the specific proposition, and all the circumstances under which it is to be brought forward, are known. This, therefore, is the main object, to keep Government from being considered as pledged in the interval, and to avoid, at this peculiar crisis, any step which could disgust our friends or loosen their support. The idea, therefore, of collecting information with regard to future proposals, and the temper of both sides,

must be, at least during this critical time, sub-
servient to the other.   I have stated it as fully
as I have done that you may see the extent of
what we wish upon the subject.   It remains for
your discretion how far such inquiries can be
carried without interfering with this principal
object, of occasioning no jealousy and alarm in
this present moment.   The conduct of the business will much depend on address and dexterity ;
but for that very reason I am persuaded whatever can be done will be done.   Let me only
add, before I quit this subject, that I should not
have given you all this trouble upon it if I did
not feel it my duty to you as well as to myself
to apprise you fairly of all that is passing in my
mind upon it.   I do not pretend to be able to
judge with certainty what the fate of the question will be here, but I think the great probability is that it will be carried.   I will let you
know as soon as the prospect is more decided,
and communicate to you as early as possible the
detail of my plan.   Give me credit, in the meantime, when I assure you, that if Ireland adopts
anything like the same model, the true interest,
both of Government and of this country, will be
safe.   You will perceive that I write all this in
the most perfect confidence.   There is nothing,
however, which I do not wish to be communicated, if you please, to Mr Orde, who is indeed

already in possession of most of these sentiments. The other great question, of the measures to be taken respecting volunteers, requires less explanation. The general line of our opinion is plainly marked; but more minute information seems necessary before any actual decision can be formed. I am inclined to think the plan for a militia should be completed and carried before anything is proposed for disbanding the volunteers. The time and mode of this latter proposal is delicate. Important and necessary as [is] the object, it may be endangered, or at least embarrassed, if too soon brought forward. Should there appear, after a certain time, a prospect that the complete arrangement of commercial questions will be followed by some satisfaction on this essential point of reform, I believe the arms will then drop out of the hands of the volunteers without a struggle, and measures to be taken effectually to prevent their being ever resumed. On this subject, however, we can give more distinct opinions when we have heard more particularly from your side of the water what mode you think on the whole most practicable. I have only now to thank you for your letters, which, though they speak of the remains of your complaint, give me hopes that you are recovering faster than you perhaps imagine. I am sorry to find you still entertained such strong

apprehensions on the idea of the contribution;
but I have already exhausted all I can say on
the subject. I trust and hope the particular
mode proposed will obviate most of your objections; and I continue firm in expecting that,
with the exertions which I am sure will be made,
every difficulty will be surmounted. Indeed we
cannot relinquish the ground. I enclose to you
a draft of resolutions, which I trust will become
waste paper. They contain what we must propose to Parliament here, if the proposal for contribution fails in the first instance. To these
declarations I would annex the resolutions (in
the shape you have them already) containing
the detail of the intended commercial [conces-
sions], and so hold out the whole system at once
to be either taken or rejected by Ireland. This
system may appear adventurous, but if we should
be reduced to the extremity of recurring to it, I
am confident it will have its effect. I shall be
impatient to hear from you, both on the subject
of public measures, and equally so on the progress of your recovery, which I hope and trust
will be every day more rapid. — Adieu, ever
yours,   W. PITT.

MR PITT TO THE DUKE OF RUTLAND.

DOWNING STREET, *Jan.* 11, 1785.

MY DEAR DUKE,—When the last messenger was despatched my hands were so full that I could not add to the long letter I was obliged to send you, what I have long wished to state to you, on the subject of a letter you sent me before your illness. I mean that in which you express your anxiety to procure the appointment of Vice-Treasurer, in case of any vacancy, for Lord Mornington. Your Grace thoroughly knows my desire to comply with any wish in which you seem so much interested, as well as the particular pleasure I should feel in any arrangement agreeable to Lord Mornington. The fact is, that without some opening, which I do not foresee at present, no such vacancy is likely to happen ; and if it did, there are claims and pretensions in our House of Commons which it would be impossible for me to set aside, as things stand at present. In any communication you have to make to Lord Mornington, let me beg you to do justice to the value I put, in common with yourself, on the credit and advantage of his support to Government. I shall also trouble him with a few lines, to state how I am circumstanced on the subject.—Ever, my dear Duke, most faithfully and sincerely yours,   W. PITT.

MR PITT TO THE DUKE OF RUTLAND.

[*Private.*]   PUTNEY HEATH, *Jan.* 12, 1785.

MY DEAR DUKE,—I am ashamed of troubling
you again with so voluminous a packet, but this
addition to it shall not be a long one. Having
said so much on Irish reform, you will not
wonder at seeing a few words relative to the
same subject in England, on which I trust your
sentiments are unaltered, though I am aware,
in your particular situation, you may have some
delicacy in acting upon them. I really think
that I see more than ever the chance of effecting
a safe and temperate plan, and I think its success
as essential to the credit, if not the stability, of
the present administration, as it is to the good
government of the country hereafter. A meeting is summoned in Yorkshire for this business.
I wish Mr Wyvill had been a little more sparing
of my name in inviting it; but I am persuaded
the friends to reform there are disposed to give
every countenance to what I shall bring forward;
at present their resolutions will probably be quite
general. I think it is very material, as the question is brought forward, that it should have all
possible strength and credit. If, therefore, you
see no objection, and would have the goodness

to promote it with any of your Yorkshire friends, it may be very useful. There is another point of view which makes the attendance of our friends very material. Unpopular as the coalition interest is in Yorkshire, they may, perhaps, nevertheless endeavour to raise a cry against our window tax, or other measures, which, though I am fully satisfied of their good effects, are not, in the moment, favourites without doors. Two persons are particularly named to me, to whom a word from your Grace might be useful; the first is Croft, who, though attached to you, and a friend to the reform, is, with his family, a supporter of the Fitzwilliam interest. Possibly you may confirm him in the first sentiment, and keep him from joining his other friends in any hostile measures. The other is Mr Bell, of Thirsk, who is stated to be a person of great weight, and likely to be influenced by any intimation of your wishes. You know, my dear Duke, whether you can with propriety take any step towards either of these, but your zeal and friendship will, I am sure, forgive my suggesting it ; and if you can do anything in it I shall be greatly obliged to you. I really have the whole of this subject inexpressibly at heart. — Ever most faithfully yours, W. PITT.

MR PITT TO MR ORDE.

PUTNEY HEATH, *Jan.* 12, 1785.

MY DEAR SIR,—I enclose the drafts you left with me of the speech and address, and have, as you desired, made such alterations as occurred to me in considering them. Having no one here whom I like to employ in copying them, I send them in a very rough state. At all events the words I have suggested will require much correction. The principal object I have had in view, and which I think material, is this : that there should be no expressions which should be supposed to convey a general disapprobation of agitating the question of reform (providing it is done decently and peaceably), or which could be construed as adverse to the right of meeting to petition and to consult upon grievances.

It is essential, for reasons I have stated often to you, and repeated in a letter to the Duke, which he will no doubt show you, that Government should not commit itself in Ireland while the question of reform is undecided here. The same reason operates still more strongly for not letting Parliament be prematurely pledged on the subject. Partly from the same motive, and from some other strong ones, it will be very desirable to abstain from any direct proceedings against the assembly of delegates, if they meet. It is certainly true, and is an argument which ought to satisfy our most zealous and sanguine friends, that the taking notice of them in Parliament will give them a consequence they can probably have no other way, and may be the means of raising a flame in the country. I have written so much at large to the Duke, that I will not tire you with any repetition. I am impatient to hear the result of your communication with the leading parliamentary interests, and with the Speaker. I do trust it is impossible that by objecting to the contribution they will destroy the whole chance of the settlement which every hour convinces me must be the consequence. I rely upon your goodness to find half an hour to let me know minutely what each of the great chieftains, such as Lord Shannon, &c., have said to it. I know how much your time is taken up. Only be so good to write, without any ceremony, whatever occurs, of which I am sure in this letter I venture to set you the example. In what I wrote last time to the Duke, I stated why I conceived it impossible that anything more than a general account of the money paid on the proposed contribution should be laid before the Irish Parliament. I am confirmed in thinking that anything more would let them into a control on the executive government of the empire, which must *completely* reside here. That point, therefore, seems essential. I omitted to mention what is, perhaps, as important to the object. You will consider on the spot what can be done. The point I mean is one that we often mention in our conversations, though it was never reduced to writing; that is, how to secure the hereditary revenue from being *diminished by further additional duties on the articles* that pay to it. I apprehend such additions would not, in fact, be likely, but for this very object; and the natural way to prevent it seems to be, by agreeing that any addition to the principal articles (if made) *shall go to the hereditary revenue, and not to any other fund.* I have had some conversation with your Attorney-General on the subject of the attachments, who defends his cause very ably, and puts it in the best light it can admit of. Still I think it is a matter of great delicacy and caution, and enough has been done already. It would certainly be fortunate if the Leitrim business can be got rid of. I shall hope to hear from you before long, and to learn, in the first place, that the substance of what we wish is fully agreed to; and also in what form the resolutions, particularly concerning the contribution, are to be proposed. We must, according to our present idea, wait for your resolutions being passed in Ireland before we propose ours here. On the subject of lowering duties, we are getting more information respecting woollens and the other chief articles. I continue to think we may rest satisfied with the proposed rate of duties, and I hope to be able to write decisively in a few days. The question of *full drawbacks* on foreign goods going from one country to the other is also yet undecided, but that, I trust, may accompany the other. In our fourth resolution, concerning the manufacture of either country exported from the other, I am apprehensive there is an inaccuracy in what is said of the drawback. The effect, as it now stands, would be, that Irish cottons (for example), though paying *more duty* than our own, would be entitled only to the *same drawback;* whereas I think the intention must have been that they should go out *equally free* from duty. This, however, deserves inquiry and consideration.— I am, with great truth and regard, my dear Sir, sincerely yours, W. PITT.

I hope you will be able soon to furnish me with the state of parliamentary interests which you took to complete.

.

MR PITT TO THE DUKE OF RUTLAND.

[*Private.*]   DOWNING STREET,
Wednesday night, Jan. 19, 1785.

MY DEAR DUKE,—I will detain this messenger
no longer than to thank you most heartily for
your letter. The zeal and spirit with which you
undertake the great work depending, in spite of
seeming difficulties, is the best pledge for over-
coming them. I trust every hour will forward
your recovery, and that you are much more than
equal by this time to the fatigue of to-morrow's
ceremony.[1] We shall be all impatient to hear
of you again as soon as possible. The few small
points on which any farther explanation is wanting from hence, we shall be able to clear up
before the time that any steps are to be taken
in your Parliament. I will write to you again
very soon.—In the meantime adieu, and believe
me always most truly and affectionately yours,

W. PITT.

MR PITT TO THE DUKE OF RUTLAND.

DOWNING STREET, *Feb.* 1, 1785.

MY DEAR DUKE, — I have troubled you so
much that I wish to make my letter now as

---

[1] The opening of the Irish Parliament.

short as I can. Lord Sydney's official despatch, and a letter I have written to Orde, a good deal longer than I intended, exhaust all I can say on the great public subjects. I am sure I need not entreat you to exert every effort in carrying the most favourable of the alternatives recommended, and not driving us, if it can be avoided, to accept the contribution in the shape the least creditable and satisfactory. I will therefore say no more on this business, but wait with eagerness for the result.

The enclosed letter from Lord Buckingham will in some measure speak for itself. I can only add, that I recollect perfectly discourse on the subject of Gardiner's pretensions, but I have no distinct recollection of any authority for a specific promise. However, I had so many things in my mind that I do not entirely trust my memory ; and if there is a doubt I feel most truly anxious to stand on the clearest grounds. I think, too, the history of his pretensions so strong, that they have a claim to be attended to as soon as possible. I cannot judge how far it is possible for you, without inconvenience, to include him now ; and with the whole transaction before you it is entirely for you to decide. I shall on no account, where I can avoid it, press any man's request on you, but I am anxious for anything like an engagement to which we are

either of us parties. I must, however, add, that
if the peerage should be extended in any one
instance it would be impossible not to include
Mr Stuart,[1] for whom Lord Camden makes a
great point, though he will not absolutely press
it if there are no new recommendations.

I rejoice to hear of the progress of your recovery, and congratulate you on your successful
opening.[2] — Believe me ever, my dear Duke,
most faithfully yours,   W. PITT.

(*Enclosure.*)

THE MARQUESS OF BUCKINGHAM TO MR PITT.

January 23, 1785.

MY DEAR PITT,—I have been anxiously turn-
ing in my mind the whole day the means of
parrying what may be unpleasant to you ; and
I had conceived hopes of a solution, which is
destroyed by one of the names, and would be
more completely so by any other names than
those of Sir C. Maude and Mr O'Callaghan.
These gentlemen stand first in the Duke of
Portland's official list ; and if your creations
had stopped there, I might have made an ex-

[1] Robert Stewart, created in 1789 Baron Londonderry, in 1795
a Viscount, in 1796 Earl, and in 1816 Marquess.
[2] Of the Irish Parliament.

cusc, certainly very shuffling, yet such as my earnest wish to facilitate your ideas would have driven me to adopt, sorely against my feelings. At present I own that I am at a loss, and you must recommend to the Duke of Rutland to consider—

That a peerage was promised to Mr G. by the Earl of Bucks in 1779.

That this promise was confirmed by the Earl of Carlisle, and verbally discharged by Mr Eden, who recommended him, as appears by a letter from Lord Carlisle to Mr Gardiner.

That the Duke of Portland, in a letter (now in the office) dated Aug. 5, to Mr Secretary Townshend, recommends him for a peerage.

That Lord Temple confirmed this engagement in 1782, when he had his Majesty's permission to recommend for peerages *whenever the Parliament met.*

That this promise, and that to Lord Chief Baron Burgh, was acknowledged by Lord Northington, but refused by him, by which refusal Mr Gardiner was driven into opposition, in which he embarked in the business of protecting duties, &c.

That upon the change of Government I was desired to converse with him upon the subject of those motions, and specifically to throw out the idea of his attaining his object, it being then deemed essential to check that question, to which his name and credit gave much support. I certainly held myself authorised to hold it out to him in case of his support, which he promised; stating, however, that he had pledged himself to move that question after the recess, but that he would take the first moment to quit it, and to return to that system from which he had been driven by Lord Northington. It is difficult to recollect precise words, but I do not doubt that I left the impression of certain success upon his mind, because that is the impression which now remains upon mine; nor do I conceive that he will admit his conduct upon the protecting duties to be a reason for what he will term a breach of faith in the moment in which you are doing almost exactly the very thing which he proposed. In all events it will leave me in a most unpleasant situation; and in the moment in which the Government of Ireland is fulfilling engagements, I am sure that the Duke will recollect that none press upon him from me, and that no considerations but those of his ease and yours could have induced me, with his knowledge, to this communication with Gardiner. Think over this, my dear Pitt, and refer it in whatever way you think best to the Duke. I would have written to him myself, but that I do not like to press upon his friendship what in fact is a measure of Government, uninteresting to me upon every other ground than that of jealousy for my faith, which Mr G. conceives pledged, and which I cannot disavow, and to plead misconception will disgrace both you and me.[1]—Ever yours,   NUGENT BUCKINGHAM.

MR PITT TO THE DUKE OF RUTLAND.

[*Most private.*]   DOWNING STREET, *Feb.* 24, 1785.

MY DEAR DUKE,—At this anxious moment I am sorry the pressure of other business, and the importance of the questions to be decided on, has made it impossible for us to despatch this messenger sooner.   You will see by Lord Sydney's despatch how we all feel on the business.   Be assured, however, of our firm persuasion that you made no concession but what at the moment of the decision you thought necessary, and conducive to the general object. You must, at the same time, allow for the absolute impossibility of our maintaining this system, while so essential a part is left in any respect disputable.   Though you may have reason enough to confide in the intention of the Irish Parliament to make the principle

[1] Mr Gardiner obtained the title of Viscount Mountjoy, and was father of the late Earl of Blessington.

effectual under the resolutions as altered, yet
recollect how impossible it is, in a final agree-
ment between two nations, that the stipula-
tions should not be made equally secure on
both sides.   We consider the resolutions as
they have been passed in Ireland as a recogni-
tion of the principle which we think essential.
It has been argued upon here as such.   But it
is *absolutely necessary* to the success of the
whole plan, and to the general interest of our
Government, to get rid some way or other of
the doubt arising from the condition added to
the resolution.   I think it is perfectly possible,
upon its being understood that everything depends upon it, that the Irish Parliament will
give the necessary explanation without difficulty.   For all our sakes, and for that of both
countries, I earnestly hope that will be the
case, as without it this great work has not a
chance of success.   All we ask of Ireland is to
clear from doubt and uncertainty a principle
which they must consider themselves as having
assented to.   If Ireland has meant fairly in the
resolutions which have been passed, they will
in effect gain nothing by the limitation introduced, because the surplus will as much go to
us as if the grant had been absolute.   I see,
therefore, little or no awkwardness in their
taking the measures necessary to remove this

difficulty. Whether any explanatory resolutions can be brought forward now, or whether it is best to wait till you are fortified by the declarations of our Parliament, you must judge on the spot. Either now, or after that resolution, the thing must be obtained, or the whole arrangement given up. It will undoubtedly be pleasanter to us to have the points as stated in Lord Sydney's despatch cleared up immediately; but the attempt should not be prematurely hazarded, if you suppose that it will be more easy to carry it after the resolution which is transmitted to you shall have been passed here. In the meantime I can only add, that on this point the sense, both of Parliament and the nation, is decided, that if we fail in this everything we have hoped for is suspended. What the consequence finally may be, it is impossible to guess; but there is no one contingency which can make us think ourselves warranted to depart from the determination now formed. I trust and hope the issue of it will relieve both you and us from all farther anxiety upon it, and render the success you have a prospect of in other measures worth congratulation. I am happy to hear you are gaining so much ground in your health.—Ever faithfully yours,

W. PITT.

MR PITT TO THE DUKE OF RUTLAND.

Tuesday Night, March 1, 1785.
DOWNING STREET.

MY DEAR DUKE,—Mr Cooke arrived here this morning with your despatch. I have at this time but a moment, and I trust very little interval will elapse before you hear from us more fully. In the meanwhile, I have great satisfaction in being confirmed by Mr Cooke's statement in the opinion I have before conceived, that the Parliament of Ireland mean the fair and complete execution of the principle in question. Our objection is, solely, that in the mode proposed the surplus was rendered dependent upon the disposition and humour of the Irish from time to time. If this objection can be removed, and at the same time a pledge be secured to Ireland for an economical conduct in the Irish Government, we should be far from feeling it any embarrassment to the scheme. But it is essential that the contingency should not be left dependent on the opinions or interests that may prevail from time to time. I think I see daylight as to the possibility of reconciling these objects; I am sure the same zeal and firmness which has carried you through your other difficulties, will determine you to make every exertion to settle this in a way satisfactory to both countries. We are all embarked in the same cause, and can have but one wish upon it, for the advantage of the public service, and the credit of all parts of the Government. Nothing shall be wanting on our parts to accommodate the line we take to your situation and circumstances, by every means consistent with the essential principle which is the foundation of the whole plan, and on which alone it can be justified. This point happily settled, all other difficulties will, I am sure, speedily vanish. I rejoice to hear so good an account of your health.—Ever, my dear Duke, most faithfully and affectionately yours,   W. PITT.

MR PITT TO THE DUKE OF RUTLAND.

PUTNEY HEATH, *April* 2, 1785.

MY DEAR DUKE,—I was extremely glad last year to be able, though it was not without much embarrassment and difficulty, to give Mr Francis the appointment of Receiver-General for Cambridgeshire, as you desired; but it was expressly understood by Mr Mortlock at the time, that his appointment could not be continued beyond the year; and I am under such strong engagements, made before your Grace first applied, that I have

no option left, if Mr Yorke claims my promise.
This makes it unnecessary to trouble you with
any other circumstances relative to this business,
as you will see that, unfortunately, it is not in
this instance possible for me to comply, as I
always wish to do, with what you desire.—Ever,
my dear Duke, your faithful and affectionate
friend,   W. PITT.

THE DUKE OF RUTLAND TO MR PITT.

[*Private.*]   DUBLIN CASTLE, *May* 19, 1785.

MY DEAR PITT,—I congratulate you most sincerely on the very powerful majority by which
you have established your question on the Irish
propositions. You may depend upon it that I
will do my part to the best of my power; but I
must fairly tell you that the alterations, which
(in compliance, I suppose, with the prejudices of
England) you have found it expedient to make
from the original form of the adjustment, will
render it very unpalatable to Ireland, and impose on me a task of extreme difficulty to
prevent the operation and triumphs of faction.
I have not yet considered the different alterations so attentively, nor have I yet seen persons
sufficient to state to you precisely how far I shall
be able to reconcile people's minds to many of
them. But on one point which I find to be

contained in the body of the resolutions, I mean that which relates to the perpetuity of the laws for the collection of the revenue, I will not attempt to deceive you, but at once pronounce it impossible to be carried. Be assured Mr Orde would enter the House with scarce a man to support him on such a question; and when you are convinced of its failure (which, upon my honour, would be its fate), you will scarcely judge it to be wise to persist in an odious measure, on which the credit, the reputation, the strength, and even the existence of the King's Government is to be staked, without the smallest probability of success. Believe me, I have not overcharged the picture, nor have placed the difficulties in too strong a point of view; and were propositions ten times as advantageous to be offered, with this obnoxious clause annexed, I am convinced the country would reject them. When I can state to you with more precision the temper of the country, and how far the deviation from the original tenor of the propositions is likely to be received, you shall hear from me again. At the same time you may rest assured of my most zealous exertions to bring matters of such importance to the cause in which we are embarked, and to the lasting advantage of the empire, to a happy conclusion. —I am, &c., RUTLAND.

P.S.—I am glad the words of your resolutions do not precisely express the necessity of passing *perpetual laws.* Secure provisions of satisfactory permanency, perhaps, may be obtained, and even possibly the regulations might be made perpetual, but the severe penal laws are out of the question.

MR PITT TO THE DUKE OF RUTLAND.

PUTNEY HEATH, *May* 21, 1785.

MY DEAR DUKE,—I mentioned to you some time since that Lord Mulgrave had expressed an earnest wish to be included in the Irish peers advanced to earldoms. I understood that you were apprehensive of being embarrassed by it, and communicated that to him, in which he very handsomely acquiesced. A circumstance has arisen since which has induced him to renew it with more earnestness. He understands that Lord Glerawley is on the list, and Lord Glerawley has applied to him to know whether he would object to his having the title of Anglesey, to the former possessors of which Lord Mulgrave conceives himself to be the most nearly allied. I do not recollect whether Lord Glerawley is on the list; nor do I know the exact state of the different claims to the title in question. But I perceive that Lord Mulgrave is very anxious on this subject, and I am very desirous, as far as possible, to assist him; though, certainly, not wishing to press it, if it seems to you likely to produce any considerable inconvenience. He states that many peers have been made over his head, and that the promotion is now meant to take in Lord Longford, between whom and himself there are very few barons, and none that seem to have any pretensions at present.—I am ever, my dear Duke, sincerely yours,   W. PITT.

I have received your letter relative to Mr Francis, and am much obliged to you for waiving the former point. I believe there is hardly a precedent of dividing in such cases the receipt of the window duty from the land tax; but I will inquire, and write to you as soon as I know what I am at liberty to do.

MR PITT TO THE DUKE OF RUTLAND.

[*Most private.*]   PUTNEY HEATH, *May* 21, 1785.

MY DEAR DUKE,—I understand by a letter which Mr Rose received yesterday morning from Mr Orde, that you would despatch a messenger with an answer to my former letter on Thursday

or Friday. I do not wait his arrival, because
there are some points on which I am anxious to
write fully to you without loss of time. By the
nature of what I have to say you will perceive
it to be in absolute confidence between you and
me, and meant only for your private perusal;
though I trust it will appear to you to be
of weight in influencing the public measures of
which you have the guidance. I find Mr Orde
alarmed at our insisting on perpetuating the laws
for the collection of the revenue, and apprehensive of the effects of other amendments. You will,
I am sure, give me credit, my dear Duke, from
every motive, public and private, for wishing to
smooth the way to this great settlement as much
as possible. Its speedy and prosperous conclusion interests me in every point of view; and to
diminish your share of difficulties I trust you
will think is not a matter of indifference to me.
But, really, this point does appear to me, both in
itself and from the combination of circumstances,
absolutely indispensable. The grounds have
been often explained, and in a letter I have
now written to Mr Orde, I have repeated many
of them. But, besides this, we are committed
in the eye of the public, by a resolution deliber-
ately brought forward after an interval of two
months; and we cannot recede without giving
an advantage against us that we might never

recover. Do not imagine, because we have had two triumphant divisions, that we have everything before us. We have an indefatigable enemy, sharpened by disappointment, watching and improving every opportunity. It has required infinite patience, management, and exertion to meet the clamour without doors, and to prevent it infecting our supporters in the house. Our majority, though a large one, is composed of men who think, or at least act, so much for themselves, that we are hardly sure from day to day what impression they may receive. We have worked them up to carry us through this undertaking in its present shape; but we have had awkwardness enough already in many parts of the discussion. The idea of having stirred this question first in Ireland, without taking previously the sense of the Parliament of England; the necessity we have been under to make explanations and amendments (which, though perfectly consistent with the general tenor of the original resolutions, are for this purpose magnified and misrepresented by opposition); the inference attempted to be drawn from hence, that the propositions were not at first properly considered; and the argument drawn for farther delay, from stating the danger which would have followed if they had been passed as we first proposed them; all these topics, enforced and aggravated as you will imagine them, have damped, and, perhaps, in some instances discontented our friends, even in the moment of victory. Any new circumstance of embarrassment might have the effect, sooner than can almost be imagined, of reversing our apparent situation of strength and security. It would give a credit to the invidious attacks of opposition, and a turn to the general opinion which we should not know how to counteract. I assure you, therefore, seriously, and upon my honour, that the carrying this point seems essential to the success of this measure, and material to all the future prospects .of Government. Knowing all you feel on this subject, I need say no more. You will, I am sure, not let any difficulty that can by possibility be surmounted involve our whole system in hazard. You are not, I am aware, without plagues and embarrassments on your side, but I believe (though on the whole I do not envy it) that you have a Parliament more manageable than ours. Your perseverance has abated, if not extinguished, the alarms without doors. On this point you are in no respect committed against it. The solid objections, in point of argument, are none. We are absolutely committed for it. The security of the contribution, on the strength of which we uphold our system, is gone without it; and, therefore, unless this can be carried, believe me, the whole settlement is at an end. As to your means of carrying it, it is difficult to judge at a distance, but I protest, if it is resolutely pushed, I can hardly conceive how you can have any formidable opposition.

Adieu, my dear Duke. I cannot describe to you the earnestness and anxiety with which I write on this subject, feeling how near we are to the attainment of so great an object, and yet how possible it is for this circumstance, comparatively small, to defeat the whole.—Believe me ever, most faithfully and affectionately yours,

W. PITT.

Be so good to destroy this letter when you have read and considered it.

THE DUKE OF RUTLAND TO MR PITT.

[*Secret and confidential.*]   PHŒNIX PARK, *July* 4, 1785.

MY DEAR PITT,—I have seen Mr Grattan, but found him impracticable in a degree scarcely credible. I desired to be apprised of his objections, and stated my reliance on your disposition to modify, as far as candour could require, those parts which were deemed exceptionable in Ireland; but his ideas of objection were such as to render them impossible to be obviated.

He said that he could admit nothing which in-
trenched on old settlements; that it seemed an
attempt to resume in peace concessions granted
in war; that rendering the fourth proposition
conditional was of but little avail; that everything should be left to national faith, and nothing covenanted. He objected to the American
and the East Indian clauses, and that which
relates to the permanent collection of the
revenue. He seemed not to think it possible,
by any explanations, to remove the difficulties,
but held firm in his opinion that anything,
except the eleven specific propositions, as they
went from Ireland, was perfectly inadmissible.
I then observed to him the ill effects which
might probably ensue from a successful opposition, and from his taking an inflammatory
part; but he only answered, that he only expected, at any rate, a very unpleasant scene of
discontent; that if the question was carried, and
the fourth proposition rendered conditional, of
course the settlement would not be final, and
that it would then be a perpetual struggle to
alter a duty, and to get rid of the whole. In
short, he appears to have adopted a decided line
of opposition, and has returned to his vomit, and
to the support of the desperate views of an
English abandoned faction in Ireland. He can
certainly create much obstruction and mischief,

but we will be prepared. Conolly has likewise joined the standard of the old party, in spite of all his affected declarations to the contrary, and Mr Daly remains sullenly in the country, without deigning to answer a letter which Mr Orde has written to him. The last defection, which was expected if the Portland interest should have the appearance of strength, will be the Ponsonby connection; but as yet they profess to support. I am still sanguine of success, if you can accomplish all those modifications and explanations which you seem disposed to concede to Irish prejudices. I beg, therefore, you may not be dismayed, nor relax your exertions to produce such a system as it will be lunacy in Ireland to refuse. If the exceptionable clauses are explained in the manner you propose, these gentlemen will have no fair ground remaining for objection, and I may say will be left without excuse if they persist in a conduct so dangerous, so destructive of the true interest of their country, and so repugnant to all the principles they have ever pretended to profess.—I am, my dear Pitt, your affectionate friend,   RUTLAND.

P.S.—Mr Grattan or Mr Conolly asserted in the House that you altered the resolutions from conviction, and not from examination or want of numbers.

MR PITT TO THE DUKE OF RUTLAND.

[*Private.*]   BURTON PYNSENT, *Aug.* 8, 1785.

MY DEAR DUKE,—I arrived here last Thursday, intending to forget, if possible, for a little while, the scene which has lasted so long, and had the mortification to find my mother recovering but slowly (though out of danger) from a complaint in her stomach of a very alarming sort, with which she was attacked about a fortnight since. She has been mending from that time ; but under these circumstances, and after two years' absence, I hardly find an hour to command here more easily than in the busy moments of London. I most devoutly hope that the shape in which we have sent our bill, and the alterations in yours to make it correspond, will prove satisfactory. We have strove to consult not only reason, but even, as far as we could, prejudice, and I know not how we can, on this side, go an inch farther. The main difficulties seem so far removed, that I can hardly see how accident or malice can raise any essential obstacles, and I hope for the best. If you succeed in the accomplishment of the great work which now rests with you, I may indeed congratulate you on the most important service which I believe can, in the existing state of things, be rendered to either kingdom.

I have a long arrear of things to say to you, and have even now hardly the leisure. You will, I am sure, have accounted for my silence from the real cause, and I must still wait an opportunity to write more fully.

I cannot omit telling you, however, that the conclusion of our session has been in all respects triumphant. The zeal of our friends seems more confirmed than ever; and everything essential to the strength of our Government as satisfactory as possible. I find rumours are spread of a spirit of disunion in the Cabinet, especially on the subject of Ireland. I can assure you, on my honour (and it is a subject on which I would on no consideration leave you in the dark), that the reverse is the truth. Whatever room for discussion there may be in the modes to be adopted, in all substantial points, and in the common cause of Government, a more cordial co-operation never existed. The newspapers are equally filled with lies on the idea of hostile appearances towards France. The state of politics on the Continent is delicate enough, but still, I believe, may be improved to our advantage, without any hazard of our being involved. And let this business of Ireland terminate well, let peace continue for five years, and we shall again look any Power in Europe in the face. In what remains to be done in Ireland, I have only to conjure you not to admit of expedients which sacrifice any part of the consistency, effect, or even appearance of the plan, to the caprices or pretences of men who either object captiously and without intending to be satisfied, or who are afraid for any object to hazard momentary unpopularity.

The fourth proposition, as explained by the address, by our bill, and by the draft of yours as we have corrected it, is essential to everything. Any attempt to fritter it down, under colour of making it more palatable, should at all events be rejected. To attempt to blink or to disguise so fundamental a point, would, in my firm belief, be as ruinous as, I am sure, it would be disgraceful. Putting it, like all the other points, *expressly* as a fundamental article of the settlement, is the only way that can be either distinct or effectual.

I meant to have added a page on the subject of individuals concerning whom you have written to me, but I must close for the present.—Yours ever most affectionately,   W. Pitt.

MR PITT TO THE DUKE OF RUTLAND.

[*Private.*] BURTON PYNSENT, *August* 8, 1785.

MY DEAR DUKE,—Before I say a word about the particular objects of different letters I have received from you, I hope I need not employ many in endeavouring to remove an impression under which one of them was written. It would be unaccountable, indeed, if, in addition to the pleasure I ought to feel whenever I can promote any wish you form, I was not sensible how much everything in which I can be interested is connected with your credit and importance. Let me beg you, therefore, to believe that it is not for want of this conviction if it ever happens that I am under the necessity of postponing any object you recommended. You will, I am sure, make allowances for the innumerable calls on a limited patronage; but when there is any object out of the line of the ordinary claims to which you are bound to give attention, in which you have a real and personal wish, or which you think of importance to your own views, *if* I know it in time it shall not be disappointed. As to Sir Joshua Reynolds, the office was promised, on the pressing application of Lord Weymouth, before I had your letter.

H

Allow me, however, just to add, that his situation cannot make an office very necessary to him ; and that though he is an excellent private friend, the only part he ever has taken in anything like politics would not make his promotion tend much to your importance, or operate on the public as a very good example.   With regard to the Receivership at Cambridge, I was bound by positive promise, and the collection of the two duties could not properly be separated.   I wish much to know exactly to what point you interest yourself for Captain Molloy.   Some of the things he has looked to are not natural.   What he has last named is the government of Antigua, for himself or La Forey.   I have not had time to inquire what competitors there are, or their relative claims, but if this is a point you have strongly at heart, all shall be done that is possible ; the only thing I have to beg is, that you will let me know on what subjects you are most anxious, that they may be attended to in their due order.   There must be enough besides which I know you cannot absolutely decline, but which you must equally know I cannot speedily satisfy.   I need add nothing on political subjects to what I wrote last night, and you will, I am persuaded, find in your own mind all the firmness and resolution which, at the point at which things now are, can alone ensure your credit or the general success.   Farther relaxation is absolutely out of the question.—Ever faithfully and affectionately yours,   W. PITT.

I do not know whether you have yet heard anything of my brother.   He is at present at Buxton with Lady Chatham, who was much recovered before she went, and is, I hope, making a further progress.

THE DUKE OF RUTLAND TO MR PITT.

DUBLIN CASTLE, *August* 13, 1785.

MY DEAR PITT,—I am most extremely concerned to inform you, that after a tedious debate, which continued till past nine in the morning, the House came to a division, when the numbers for admitting the bill were 127 to 108.   You may well imagine that so small a majority as nineteen on so strong a question as the admission of the bill affords no great hopes as to the ultimate fate of the measure.   It will be an effort of our united strength to get the bill printed, that at least it may remain as a monument of the liberality of Great Britain, and of my desire to promote a system which promises such essential advantage to the empire.   All my influence must likewise be exerted on Monday to defeat a

motion from Mr Flood, to the purpose of declar-
ing " the four propositions, as passed in the Parliament of Great Britain, as destructive of the
liberties and constitution of Ireland." Such a
declaration is of a nature too hostile to be en-
dured for a moment. The speech of Mr Grattan was, I understand, a display of the most
beautiful eloquence perhaps ever heard, but it
was seditious and inflammatory to a degree
hardly credible. The theory and positions laid
down both in his speech and that of Mr Flood
amounted to nothing less than war with England. This was distinctly told him in so many
words by Mr Pole. The Attorney-General supported me in the most honourable and manly
manner, and has committed himself without reserve. Our only line left is to force, if possible,
the bill to be read, and then to adjourn, that men
may have time to return to their senses. It
grieves me to think that a system which held
out so much advantage to the empire, and which
was so fair between the two countries, should
meet a fate so contrary to its deserts; and I may
say Ireland will have reason to repent her folly
if she persists in a conduct so dangerous, so destructive of her true interest, and repugnant to
every principle of connection between herself and
Great Britain. I have only to add, that I still
do not absolutely despond; but, be the event

what it may, no alteration shall take place in my determination; I will never think of quitting my station while I can render an iota of strength to your Government, or to the great cause in which we are embarked. I will write more fully after Monday. I was up all last night, and am quite worn out.—Believe me to be, ever yours,

RUTLAND.

MR PITT TO THE DUKE OF RUTLAND.

PUTNEY HEATH, *August* 17, 1785.

MY DEAR DUKE, — I confess myself not a little disappointed and hurt in the account brought me to-day by your letter and Mr Orde's of the event of Friday. I had hoped that neither prejudice nor party could on such an occasion have made so many proselytes against the true interests of the country; but the die seems in a great measure to be cast, at least for the present. Whatever it leads to, we have the satisfaction of having proposed a system, which, I believe, will not be discredited even by its failure, and we must wait times and seasons for carrying it into effect. I think you judge most wisely in making it your plan to give the interval of a long adjournment, as soon as the bill has been read and printed. With so doubtful a majority, and with so much industry to raise a spirit of opposition without doors, this is not the moment for pressing farther. It will remain to be seen whether, by showing a firm and unalterable decision to abide by the system in its present shape, and by exerting every effort both to instruct and to influence the country at large into a just opinion of the advantages held out to them, a favourable change may be produced in the general current of opinion before the time comes for resuming the consideration of the bill. I am not at all sanguine in my expectations of your division on the intended motion on Monday last. Though an opposition frequently loses its advantage by attempting to push it too far, yet on such a question, and with the encouragement of so much success, I rather conclude that absurdity and faction will have gained a second triumph; but I am very far from thinking it impossible that reflection and discussion may operate a great change before the time which your Parliament will probably meet after the adjournment. I very much wish you may at least have been just able to ward off Flood's motion, lest its standing on the journals should be an obstacle to farther proceedings at a happier moment. It is still almost incomprehensible to me, who can have been the deserters who reduced our force so low, and I wait with great impatience for a

more particular account.   All I have to say, in
the meantime, is very short; let us meet what
has happened, or whatever may happen, with
the coolness and determination of persons who
may be defeated but cannot be disgraced, and
who know that those who obstruct them are
greater sufferers than themselves.   You have only
to preserve the same spirit and temper you have
shown throughout in the remainder of this difficult scene.   Your own credit and fame will be safe,
as well as that of your friends.   I wish I could say
the same of the country you have been labouring
to serve.   Our cause is on too firm a rock here
to be materially shaken, even for the·time, by
this disappointment; and when the experience of
this fact has produced a little more wisdom in
Ireland, I believe the time will yet come when
we shall see all our views realised in both
countries, and for the advantage of both.   It
may be sooner or later, as accident, or, perhaps,
(for some time), malice may direct, but it will be
right at last.   We must spare no human exertion
to bring forward the moment as early as possible,
but we must be prepared also·to wait for it on
one uniform and resolute ground, be it ever so
late.   It will be no small consolation to you, in
the doubtful state of this one important object,
that every other part of the public scene affords
the most encouraging and animating prospect;

and you have, above all, the satisfaction of knowing that your government has made a more vigorous effort (whatever be its ultimate success) than I believe any other period of Irish history will produce, since the present train of government has been established. I write this as the first result of my feelings, and I write it to yourself alone.—Believe me ever, your most affectionate and faithful friend,   W. PITT.

P.S.—I would write to Orde, but I am fearful of detaining the messenger, and I should only repeat much of what I have said here. Will you have the goodness to tell him the cause of my not immediately answering his letter.

THE DUKE OF RUTLAND TO MR PITT.

Private.]   DUBLIN CASTLE, *August* 17, 1785.

MY DEAR PITT,—I have judged it necessary to send Mr Cooke to England (who will deliver this) to give you a particular and distinct account of our affairs in this country, and of the peculiar concurrence of embarrassing circumstances which have obliged me to postpone the consideration of the bill to a future session, rather than to risk its defeat, which, on a calculation of our numbers, was reduced to a certain event.

It has afforded me infinite concern that a
system which promised such mutual and lasting
advantages, and which by your perseverance and
exertion had been brought so near a prosperous
conclusion, should on a sudden fail after it was
committed to my conduct; but the arts which
had been too successfully practised by a desperate
and unprincipled faction have so disordered and
besotted the understandings of the nation, and
have so completely for the present destroyed
their distinguishing faculty, that they are taught
to call bitter sweet and sweet bitter. The unfortunate delays which arose in the various
stages of this business, and obstructed its quick
decision, gave opportunity for these machina-
tions to take effect; and your inability to abide
by the original tenor of the propositions had
altogether so influenced the country that to
venture on the question in its present temper
would have been an act of perfect insanity.
The business, perhaps, lay deeper than in the
mere operations of party. I have been informed,
and from some authority, that the Catholics
have likewise been active in fomenting jeal-
ousies respecting the system. I found among
many independent men that a foolish story of
Lord C.'s[1] refusal to declare his opinion on the
tendency of the fourth resolution had created

[1] Lord Charlemont ?

much alarm and distrust; in short, the current
was against it, and it would have been in vain,
in the existing state of things here, to contend
with it. At the same time, I can safely assure
you that the King's Government, which is in-
trusted in my hands, is not by any means
rendered weaker by this miscarriage, or from
the defection of those who in the hour of danger
had deserted the standard to which in a more
propitious moment they had resorted. We
had many truants, and among others, not worth
noticing, and whose names would indeed be un-
known to you, Mr Daly, very unlike himself,
was absent on the first day, which he excused
by asserting that Grattan had assured him no
opposition would take place till the commit-
ment of the bill; he appeared on the second,
in consequence of my summons, and said that
he should have contended for the admission of
the bill, but without much hope of being able
to support its principles throughout. Mr Cuffe,
though written to, and who is at the head of
the barrack board, never appeared. The Pon-
sonbys, though they thought the bill contained
many solid advantages, and objected only to
its being passed through this session against
the inflamed sense of the nation, yet declared
they could not support beyond the printing.
Their connection is very large, and would have

turned the poise of the business. Constituted in these circumstances, we are obliged to acquiesce. It becomes now a matter of consideration what steps are to be taken with those who have abandoned the Government on the important crisis. So large a body of men being involved, the question is extremely delicate; but as the delinquency of individuals rests upon different grounds, distinctions may be made; some severity, however, is rendered absolutely necessary. I beg you will be persuaded that this business has ended for this session, as well as the nature of it would admit. Misrepresented it has been, and it is not understood; but that being the case, an adjournment for six weeks or two months would not have improved it. It is now left to itself, and people will take it up at leisure, and without compulsion. The first object of the bill, the quiet of the country, is secured; and if the business should ever hereafter be resumed (and when the influence shall have subsided, of passion and of prejudice, it will be, I am persuaded, anxiously solicited), the second object will then certainly be obtained, and the final adjustment of trade between the two countries will be established.

We received a very decided and unequivocal support on this business from many material persons and connections, and it has demonstrated to me who are to be permanently depended on. The Attorney - General[1] stood forward in the most distinct and unreserved manner; Mr Pole[2], supported by his brother, Lord Mornington, took a direct line, and held a very manly language; the Provost, Mr Foster, and Mr Beresford did their part in the debate, ably and honourably; and the following of Lord Shannon, Lord Tyrone, Lord Clifden, and Lord Hillsborough were steady and decided in their support of the King's Government. Lest I should commit injustice in recapitulation, I leave it. Ask Mr Cooke, who will be able to give you every information you may require, with respect to the conduct of individuals.—I shall trouble you no longer, but to assure you, &c.

RUTLAND.

P.S.—I have received your letter respecting my private objects. It is too late to remark on that. I wish you would enable me to speak as to those claims which I have stated to you.

---

[1] The Right Hon. John Fitzgibbon, afterwards Lord Chancellor and Earl of Clare.

[2] The Right Hon. William Wellesley Pole, now Lord Maryborough.

MR PITT TO THE DUKE OF RUTLAND.

[*Secret.*]   BRIGHTHELMSTONE, *Oct.* 28, 1785.

MY DEAR DUKE,—I would not break in upon
you in the course of your tour, if the business
I wish to bring under your consideration was
less pressing and important than it is. You
will be so good to understand what I have to
say upon it as being in the most entire confidence and secrecy, as indeed the subject itself
sufficiently implies. Various accounts have
reached me from persons connected with Ireland, too material to the interest of your government, and, consequently, to us both, to make
it possible for me to delay communicating the
substance immediately to you, and desiring such
farther information and advice as you alone can
give. While all quarters agree in eulogiums,
which do not surprise me, on every part of your
own conduct, and on the prudence, spirit, and
firmness of your government, the picture they
give of the first instrument of your administration is very different. They state that Mr
Orde has incurred the imputation of irresolution
and timidity, and a suspicion even of duplicity,
still more prejudicial than his want of decision ;
and that if the management of the House of

Commons, and the duties of Secretary, are left in his hands, it will be impossible to answer what may be the consequences to Government even in the next session. This information you may imagine does not come directly to me; and I neither know how far it is to be depended upon, nor have any means myself of ascertaining it, but by stating it to you, who may be able to do so. I receive every such intimation with great allowance for a thousand prejudices or secret motives in which it may originate; but I still think it too serious to be wholly disregarded. From all I have had an opportunity of seeing, I give Mr Orde credit for considerable abilities and industry, and for perfect good intention. I am, therefore, inclined to think such representations as I have mentioned at least greatly exaggerated. But I am sensible that his manners do not lead him to be direct and explicit in doing business, and that his temper is not decisive. This may make him not distinct enough in his dealings with men or personal objects, and content, without knowing as distinctly as he ought, on the other hand, what he has to trust to from them; and these circumstances will sometimes have the appearance, and generally the bad effect, of the qualities imputed to him. It is stated particularly, that when the Commercial Bill was brought forward he had neither taken sufficient pains to ascertain who were the friends of Government, nor to collect those who were certainly so, but had trusted to vague assurances and general expectations, which produced the consequences we saw. This I am more apt to believe because I think, even now, after that session, he is not prepared to give any clear and satisfactory statement of the support on which Government may rely. I do not mention what passed on the commercial question as a thing to be lamented in the event; on the contrary, if the effect of more exertion in Mr Orde had been to procure twenty or thirty more votes in the House of Commons, it would, as events have proved, perhaps have been a misfortune; but occasions might arise in which the same want of address or vigour might be fatal. Upon the whole, if there is any reasonable ground for the suggestions I have mentioned, I think you will agree with me that it would be very desirable to open a retreat for Orde, and to endeavour to find some other person whom you would approve of to take his place. But, at the same time, this is not a resolution to be lightly taken, because, although the pledge for the continuance of the same system, and the main grounds of confidence, would still continue (where they have hitherto existed) in your own person, yet even the change of the Secretary must interrupt and derange for a time the machine of Government in a way which ought to be avoided, if there is no strong necessity for hazarding it. All, therefore, that occurs to me, under these circumstances, is, first, what I have now done, to state the whole to you, and to desire the most confidential communication of your opinions and wishes concerning it. You may, perhaps, in your situation, find it difficult to obtain from the truest friends of Government their real sentiments on so delicate a point; you may have a difficulty in endeavouring to sound any of them; and I know not whether there are any whose integrity and good sense you would trust sufficiently to communicate with them on such points; but it is possible that you may find opportunities of doing so without committing yourself too far. At all events, you can compare what I have stated with the result of your own experience and observation of Mr Orde's conduct, and you will be best able to judge whether there is any probability of its being founded. And, above all, you will have the goodness to tell me freely, whether, if (from such materials as we can collect) the opinion here should incline to remove Mr Orde, you feel in your own mind any objection provided you can pitch upon a proper person to succeed him; and be persuaded that the knowledge of your inclination in this respect will be decisive, both on my opinion and my wishes. The only other way by which I can be enabled to judge farther on this subject is by calling on Mr Orde himself (as may naturally be done in the present circumstances) to state, more precisely than he has hitherto done, the strength and reliance of Government, and the prospect he has of carrying through the public service in the House of Commons. By this means, one material part of the consideration may, I think, be ascertained with a good deal of accuracy. It may seem premature to proceed already to talk of the person to succeed before the preliminary point is ascertained. In mentioning it, however, I do not mean to anticipate your decision on the prudence of making the change (in which my own opinion is in no degree settled), but I wish, in order to avoid delay (whatever may be the final result), that the whole subject should be at once before you. I need hardly say that, if the change should take place, any person whom you could select for this trust would be sure to be at once acquiesced in here. But from what has passed formerly I must doubt whether you have any one to name, Fitzherbert being, from his situation, so far out of the question. Only three names have occurred to me, which I mention to you that you

I

may turn them in your mind. The first is
W. Grenville;[1] I do not know that he would
take it, and rather suppose that he would not.
I think, too, that his near connection with Lord
Buckingham is itself perhaps a sufficient objection, though in temper and disposition he is
much the reverse of his brother, and in good
sense and habits of business very fit for such
a situation. The second I have to name is
Steele;[2] I know as little whether he would
take it, having never hinted a syllable to him
on the subject, and I could very ill spare him
from his present situation at the Treasury; but
if no other good arrangement could be found, I
believe I should make the sacrifice, for such it
would be. He has exceeding good abilities,
great clearness and discretion, the most manly
disposition, the best temper, and most agreeable
manners possible, and speaks well in public.
The third person is Faulkener, whom I believe
you know quite as well as I do. He has the
reputation of uncommon cleverness, is very
accomplished, and seems a man of spirit. I
have had some opportunity of seeing him in
business at the Privy Council, on occasions

---

[1] William Wyndham Grenville, in 1790 created Baron Grenville.

[2] The Right Hon. Thomas Steele, for many years Secretary of
the Treasury.

which tried his abilities, and have from thence been led to rate him very high. He is, however, reckoned to be of a bad temper; but you would not be exposed to the inconvenience of it, and I should hope he would have sense enough to control it in public. I have now unbosomed myself of everything, and need not repeat that, as I have written without a shadow of reserve, all I have said is for yourself only. Have the goodness to return me an answer as speedily as you can, after revolving all this in your mind, as the season of the year requires that, one way or other, the business should be soon decided.

I have many other things to write to you upon, but this letter is too long already. I cannot conclude without telling you the pride and satisfaction I take in the credit and honour which, under all the difficulties and disappointments of the time, has resulted to yourself, and which will, I trust, be increased and confirmed in every hour of your government.—Believe me ever, my dear Duke, most faithfully and affectionately yours, W. PITT.

P.S.—I must just add (though foreign from the subject of this letter) that the situation of our finances here proves flourishing beyond almost what could be expected. We are in possession, from the existing taxes, of a surplus of about £800,000 for Sinking Fund already, and it is advancing fast to a clear million.

I should have stated that, if the change should take place, every management would be had for Orde's feelings, and it might be made to appear an act of choice in him.[1]

MR PITT TO THE DUKE OF RUTLAND.

HOLWOOD HILL, *Nov.* 13, 1785.

MY DEAR DUKE,—I have just received your letter of the 6th, and lose no time in thanking you for the full and explicit statement it contains of your opinion, and the forcible reasons in support of it. I am, be assured, infinitely happy in finding the suggestions I had thought myself obliged to communicate to you to so great a degree contradicted. Every idea of Mr Orde's retirement will be totally laid aside in my mind, unless either the result of your farther inquiries, or future events, should lead to the revival of it, which I sincerely hope and trust is highly improbable. In the meantime, my object will be, to do everything that can most

---

[1] No copy of the Duke of Rutland's reply is preserved among his papers, but from Mr Pitt's next letter it appears to have completely vindicated Mr Orde.

support his character and weight in the public opinion, and make him the most useful in his situation, by counteracting, as far as possible, the effect of the opinions which have been circulated to his disadvantage. If the issue had been his removal, I should have been equally anxious with you that it should have taken place in the way most consistent both with his feelings and his reputation. I will add no more, because I am impatient that you should receive this letter, and be assured of my hearty acquiescence and confidence in your opinion.— Believe me, faithfully and unalterably yours,

W. Pitt.

P.S.—I write from a house I have just got in Kent, where I shall pass most of my leisure between this and Christmas.

THE DUKE OF RUTLAND TO MR PITT.

[*Private.*]   Phœnix Park, *Dec.* 18, 1785.

My dear Pitt,—I congratulate you on the accession you have made to your strength, by detaching Mr Eden [1] from those with whom he had hitherto acted, and by employing him in a

---

[1] William Eden, in 1789 created Baron Auckland in Ireland, and in 1793 promoted to the British peerage.

situation where he is admirably calculated to render you material service. It strikes me to be a wise and decided measure. He is highly estimated in this country, and is considered as a man of much address and first-rate ability. I have seen letters from him, in which he speaks in the warmest terms of eulogium on your fair and honourable manner of negotiation. I know not whether he comes to you a single man, or draws to your party other connections, but at all events it is a wise measure. Everything here wears a most animating aspect; few persons are indeed as yet in town, but there appears a general determination of unequivocal support, as far as we have hitherto conversed. The appointment of consuls, protecting duties, the construction of the Navigation Act, are among the measures which the notable heads of a frustrated faction are to bring forward, by which to distress and embarrass Administration. Our conduct, as I have before observed, must be entirely defensive, except it should be deemed wise to agitate some resolution declaratory of its being unconstitutional of persons arraying to a standard without legal commissions from Government. I have assured you this string shall not be vibrated without the most explicit declarations of powerful support. But let me presume one event further, and ask your opinion;

suppose the Parliament will go fairly and honourably to this point with Government, and, in
defiance of the Legislature, the volunteers should
refuse to acquiesce in its decision, would you,
in that case, risk the attempt? My opinion
fairly is, that it should be ventured upon; but
the situation of Europe, and the general objects
of the empire, all must be taken into this consideration. When this question comes nearer
I will write to you my opinion more at large.
The present state of the funds astonishes me,
and I still look sanguinely for their increase,
when you shall give a statement of the finance
to Parliament. That alone would carry you
through all your arduous matters with victory
and triumph. Various schemes are imputed to
you for the reduction of the national debt, and
the improvement of our finances; among others,
the sale of waste lands is stated. Is there any
foundation for such an idea? You must recollect
that when I put questions of such a nature, I do
not expect to be answered. I can only assure
you of my most implicit confidence in whatever
you may adopt as a public man. I need not any
declaration of my friendship to you in private.
—Yours, &c., RUTLAND.

MR PITT TO THE DUKE OF RUTLAND.

Downing Street, *Jan.* 14, 1786.

My dear Duke,—I am ashamed of having let so many days of the new year elapse without acquitting myself of the arrears of the old one. Major Hobart has been so good to let me know he is returning, and I will not omit the opportunity of sending at least a few hasty lines. You shall hear from me more at large very soon, and I hope more punctually in future. The draft of your speech was returned yesterday by Lord Sydney, and gave entire satisfaction. I rejoice to think that your session opens without a prospect of much trouble, and we are sharers here in the same satisfaction. The acquisition we have made of Eden disarms opposition, at least as much as it exasperates them, and will tell not a little for us in the shortness of the session. I have from time to time forgot to give you an exact account of what passed between Lord Mornington and me, but I told *the result* (though not the whole of what led to it) to Orde while he was here. I found Lord Mornington full of expressions of the most cordial attachment to you, but in a different disposition towards a part of your Government, and on that account disposed to be very much out of humour. It ended, however, in the fullest declaration, on his part, of his readiness to support heartily, and on the repetition of a sincere desire on my part to open a Vice-Treasurership as speedily as possible, which I considered as distinctly engaged to him whenever it could be transferred to Ireland (the time of effecting which, I told him, could not be reduced to any certainty). All that remains is to treat him quite confidentially when he returns to Ireland, and not to let it appear, even between Orde and him, that there has ever been any misunderstanding.

Lord Macartney is arrived from Bengal, having declined (at least for a time) the post of governor-general. It is not yet clear whether he will wish to go out again, or whether we shall wish to send him. There is a good deal of discontent in India against the Act passed the year before last, which I consider as no small compliment to it. I daresay it will soon be extinguished; and as to the general state of things there, whatever present difficulties there are (which, as usual, are much magnified), the revenues are such as to make the prospect even brilliant for the future. Adieu, my dear Duke. —Ever faithfully and affectionately yours,

W. PITT.

MR PITT TO THE DUKE OF RUTLAND.

[*Private.*]   DOWNING STREET, *March* 24, [1786.]

MY DEAR DUKE, — I have long wanted to trouble you once more on the unlucky subject of the Whitby offices. You know already the embarrassment I am under from the engagement to Lord Mulgrave, which I cannot recede from. The only expedient I can find is, to prevail on him to withdraw his recommendation of the particular person obnoxious to you, and to substitute an indifferent person in his room. I must then take care of the person you interest yourself for in some other mode, and I will answer for his being completely indemnified for his disappointment, though I see now no other way out of the business, and earnestly hope you will acquiesce in this. I would not make the appointment without mentioning it to you again; and I shall wish much to hear from you upon it. I am extremely anxious, at the same time, that this whole business should be put on a footing to avoid any difficulty in future. I should be inexcusable if my first object was not to serve your interest in every way that I can with propriety. On the other hand, you will, I am sure, wish me, consistently with that object, to attend also to the just claims of other friends to Government. As to Whitby, it is an outport at some distance from Scarborough, and in the general rules of patronage offices these would not be given to the Scarborough interest, but either to the county members or to local connections; and this rule has been generally adopted in places under similar circumstances. Lord Mulgrave is so situated, from having this place at his door, that the recommendations there are an object to him beyond what they can be to any other person, and he does not consider a request for them as interfering with Scarborough, but, on the contrary, is willing to engage never to recommend any person at Whitby who belongs to Scarborough. So much as to Whitby. Besides this, he assures me in confidence that he is perfectly ready to enter into any measures that can be settled between you and him for securing your interest in Scarborough by concert, though perhaps an open junction may not be advisable. I cannot myself know what the state of parties there is; nor can I wish you to form any plan of this sort without knowing that you will strengthen your own cause by it. But if that should be the probable effect of it, you see at once how advantageous it must be, in a general view, for the strength of our Government, and how much personal ease and satisfaction I should find in

it.   You will, of course, take care not to commit
Lord Mulgrave's name to any one; but whenever you have considered the idea, and made
any inquiries you think necessary, I should be
infinitely obliged if you would let me know, in
confidence, what you think about it.   I have
written a long volume, considering the subject,
but it is one about which, for a variety of accounts, I am grown uncommonly anxious.   We
begin to look towards the end of the session, and
I find already a little respite from the load of
business, which, though lightened by its success,
has been such as to leave me hardly the leisure
to turn round, for some time past.

There are many things I want to say to you,
but those I must still defer.—Adieu, my dear
Duke, and believe me ever, sincerely and affectionately yours,   W. Pitt.

MR PITT TO THE DUKE OF RUTLAND.

[*Private.*]   Downing Street, *April* 29, 1786.

My dear Duke,—You have got completely
the start of us in the conclusion of parliamentary business.   Though we have made a very
happy progress, we have still so many points
afloat that I have with great difficulty an hour
I can call my own.   You know enough of the

unavoidable engagements added to real business, to allow for the possibility of remaining for weeks together unable to sit down with anything like leisure to write a letter. This has really been my case, or I should have been inexcusable in your not hearing from me long since. One point, particularly, I ought to have written upon; I mean the idea you communicated to me of coming for a short time to England during the recess. I am very apprehensive that fresh difficulty is now thrown in the way of it, as by the last accounts I hear that Orde is unfortunately so ill as to make his absence absolutely necessary. Under that circumstance, you would, I conceive, feel it impossible to let the government be, even for a time, under any eye but your own. If this had not happened, it seemed to me that the propriety of such a step would depend altogether upon the state of parties and of the country. If everything were reasonably quiet without doors (which I hope it is growing to be), and Government safe from any cabals either among friends or enemies, there could, I think, be no possible objection to your giving yourself relaxation, the title to which you have so well earned. I fear, however, for the reasons before mentioned, this is now out of the question; but if you wish it to be further considered, be so good to let me know. I have hitherto not mentioned it as in contemplation to any one but my brother. No official copy is yet come of your intended speech, but Lord Sydney expects it every hour. I trouble you with a separate letter on the subject of the Act brought in here respecting navigation, which I feel to be of great importance, but I think it need not be of any difficulty. We are deep in the business of Hastings, which is a great consumption of time and patience, with scarce a possibility of foreseeing the final result. We shall, however, certainly take care that it shall not much protract the session when once other public business is concluded, which will probably be within a month. I am just going to introduce a plan for excising wine, which, though it had nearly overthrown Sir Robert Walpole, will, I believe, meet with very little difficulty, though, till it is tried, I cannot speak with full confidence. A great progress is made in our French negotiation, and for your *private* information I think I may announce the prospect of a preliminary treaty to be laid before Parliament before the end of this session. The general principles of it will be for each country to place the other on the footing of the nation actually the most favoured (with an exception only for *subsisting* treaties giving any exclusive preference, as in the case of Portugal). The further abatement of duties on

specific articles will be reserved for future discussion; but this will in the meantime put an
end to all invidious and hostile distinctions, and
may possibly have a very happy effect in a
political as well as a commercial view. Care
will be taken in wording the articles to leave
Ireland a free option to participate in all the
benefits of the treaty, if the Irish Parliament
thinks proper to ratify it, or otherwise to remain
exactly in her present situation; so that I think
you can experience no difficulties in consequence.
These are, I think, the chief public points worth
troubling you with. I am very sorry to have
another piece of news to tell you, which is, that
the Chancellor [1] has been for some days so ill
as to make his situation very alarming. I
hope, however, there is a pretty good prospect
that the next account may be better, and in
the meanwhile it is desirable not to spread any
alarm, though I could not omit mentioning it
to you. I have still one subject of a private
nature to state to you, which I do with great
pain, because I am afraid it may be disagreeable
to you, and you may possibly impute the fault
to me, though I hope you will believe me when
I assure you that it is only an unavoidable
embarrassment which makes me state it to you.
The collectorship of Whitby is, as you know,

[1] Lord Thurlow.

vacant. I find you had sent to Mr Rose to desire it might not be given without your knowledge; he thought it would be time enough to mention this to me on the vacancy, and therefore delayed it. On the office falling, Lord Mulgrave came to me, and represented it as a thing at his very door, which had been before given at his *personal* recommendation, and was of the utmost importance to his situation in his own neighbourhood. On this ground I immediately promised it, and I have since the mortification to find that your friends consider it of great importance to your interest at Scarborough. I do not know how it is possible for me to recede, but I should feel more hurt than I can express if any arrangement made by me should have either the effect or the appearance of interfering with your interest. What I have earnestly to beg of you is to relieve me, if possible, from this difficulty. I trust some way might be found, of giving some office in some other place as valuable, or more so, to the person, whoever he is, whom you would recommend on this occasion; and if it is understood that such an arrangement is satisfactory to you, there can then be no misconstruction. I will readily undertake to find such an arrangement, which can probably require but little time, and will keep the other office open till

it is settled to your satisfaction. I am sorry
to have so unpleasant a business to trouble you
with. I trust to your friendship to extricate
me as well as you can. At all events, let me
hear soon.—Believe me ever, my dear Duke,
most sincerely and affectionately yours,

W. PITT.

MR PITT TO THE DUKE OF RUTLAND.

DOWNING STREET, *April* 29, 1786.

MY DEAR DUKE,—I am sorry to learn that
any difficulty has arisen relative to passing an
Act in Ireland, similar to that introduced here
for enforcing the navigation laws. I apprehend
it is impossible, as long as it is thought a privi-
lege for Irish ships to be on the same footing
as British, that any man in Ireland can object
to adopting such regulations as we think necessary for securing those exclusive privileges in
the fullest manner to the British dominions. It
would, therefore, be indispensable that your
Grace should apprise the friends of Government
in Ireland of the necessity of passing such a
bill ; and if the expectation of the conclusion of
the session makes it impossible to pass it now,
it must at least be fully understood that it is to
be proposed, and *carried without delay*, in the
beginning of the next session. If we receive

K

these assurances, some clause may perhaps with *propriety* be introduced which shall prevent the bill having any operation in excluding Irish shipping during the interval. I understand that such a clause as it is thought will answer the purpose is intended to be sent to us from Ireland, which we shall be anxious to receive and consider as soon as possible. I wish also, to prevent any uneasiness which might otherwise possibly arise, to apprise your Grace that the word *Ireland* as it stands in the second clause has been introduced inadvertently; it ought to be omitted there, and will be struck out in the committee, as it might seem to imply that the new regulations would by our Act take effect in Ireland; a thing which I certainly need not add was never intended. All we can do with propriety is to make regulations *in our Acts* to be observed in our own ports; but we certainly have a right to expect that Ireland, if she wishes her ships to continue to be deemed British, should adopt, *by her own Act,* similar regulations to be *observed in her ports.*

This is the whole substance of what is now proposed; and it seems to me so simple and reasonable, that I cannot conceive it should occasion a doubt in the mind of any one man in Ireland.—I am ever, my dear Duke, most faithfully and sincerely yours, W. PITT.

P.S.—I ought to add, that the importance of this bill is here universally felt, and so much approved of by every description of people that it would be impossible to delay it. The bill was necessarily brought in in haste. When it has been corrected in the committee, another copy shall be sent to you.

MR PITT TO THE DUKE OF RUTLAND.

DOWNING STREET, *May* 5, 1786.

MY DEAR DUKE,—A bill is now depending in the House of Commons here, for continuing in part, and subject to some new regulations, certain bounties granted some years ago on ships fitted out for the Greenland fishery. Those bounties extended to ships fitted out in Ireland; and we are willing that these should be extended in the same manner, if you think it will be acceptable. In that case, however, it is evidently necessary that Irish ships, to entitle themselves to the bounty, should conform to the conditions prescribed for ships of this country. A clause has been prepared for this purpose, which I enclose. I shall be glad to learn your sentiments as early as possible, both on the idea of including ships of Ireland on the same terms as those of this country, and on the form of the

proposed clause.   We shall take care to leave
this point open till I receive your answer, which
I therefore wish as speedily as possible.   If any
difficulty should arise relative to the condition,
which I see no reason, however, to apprehend,
the only alternative will be to confine the
bounty to ships of this country, and leave Ireland, in this respect, to take care of itself.—I
am, my dear Duke, ever faithfully and affectionately yours,   W. PITT.

P.S.—I shall enclose a copy of the bill as soon
as it is brought in.

MR PITT TO THE DUKE OF RUTLAND.

DOWNING STREET, *May* 7, 1786.

MY DEAR DUKE,—I am ashamed to find that
I omitted, by mistake, to enclose the proposed
clause relative to the Greenland fishery, which
was the subject of my last letter.   I now supply
the omission, and have time to do no more, but
will write to you again soon.   I hope to be able
to prove that I am not quite as criminal, even
towards you, as Lord North.   I do assure you,
my conscience does not accuse me of any one
voluntary neglect.   Adieu!—Ever yours,
                              W. PITT.

P.S.—You will have observed by a former letter of mine that the expedient you propose, relative to the Register Bill, meets very much our ideas. I shall trouble you upon it more particularly very soon.

MR PITT TO MR ORDE.

[*Private.*]   *July* 14, 1786.

MY DEAR SIR,—Being out of town, and not likely to return till Tuesday, I write to let you know that I have spoken to the King on the subject of the Irish creations. None will appear in the Gazette till we have had an opportunity of talking again on that subject; but I think, upon reflection, that it would on many accounts have a better effect here, and I should think answer your purpose more effectually in Ireland, if we could revert to the original idea of the Irish Marquisates, instead of the English Baronies; otherwise, not only Lord Antrim and Lord Drogheda, which is comparatively of little consequence, but Lord Hillsborough will feel himself excluded from a mark of favour, and will probably still push for the Marquisate. If any have it, Lord Shannon and Lord Tyrone, though Barons here, will not like to be passed over in their own peerage, and we shall ulti-

mately be driven to gratify them in both points.
As the idea of the English Barony was originally
suggested only as an expedient instead of the
Marquisate, I imagine you can be under no difficulty, if the King consents to the latter. One
of the two ought, I think, to take place soon, if
possible; and, as it strikes me at present, the
Irish Marquisates will be much the least objec-
tionable. I wish, however, to know what you
think of it.—I am, my dear Sir, most sincerely
yours,   W. PITT.

MR PITT TO THE DUKE OF RUTLAND.

[*Most private.*]   DOWNING STREET, *July* 19, 1786.

MY DEAR DUKE,—I find from several of your
letters that you intend to write more particularly
on the subject of the British Baronies for Lord
Shannon and Lord Tyrone, and I understand
from Mr Orde that you are exceedingly anxious
they should take place immediately. I am certainly very anxious to forward anything you
think material for the ease and success of your
government, and extremely inclined to concur
in showing a marked attention to its stedfast
supporters; but I have no difficulty in stating
fairly to you, that a variety of circumstances
have unavoidably led me to recommend a larger

addition to the British peerage than I like, or than I think quite creditable, and that I am on that account very desirous not to increase it now farther than is absolutely necessary. I am afraid, too, that the effect would be still worse here of any addition of persons possessing no property in this country, and that it would therefore come with a peculiar ill-grace just now, when there is some disposition to complain of the multiplication of honours. I fear, too, that the door being once opened will occasion great difficulty in future in any time of pressure, both to the Irish Government and to this. On the whole, therefore, I am extremely anxious that these creations (for which no precise time was ever engaged) should at least be delayed till another opportunity. But what I should like much better, on full consideration, and what I should hope would answer, not only as well, but better, on your side the water, would be, to revert to the original idea in the room of which this was substituted; I mean the creation of Marquisates. As that was the original object of Lord Shannon and Lord Tyrone, and the other only suggested as an expedient, I think they cannot complain if their first wish is gratified, especially if you approved of it. The Marquisates might be given them immediately, and they would prefer that honour at present to the

future prospect of the other. Another advantage of this arrangement would be, that Lord
Hillsborough would be included in the creation
of Marquesses ; whereas, if the others were made
Barons, he would be dissatisfied at being totally
passed over, or, perhaps, we should be driven at
last into the creation of Marquesses, after having done the other. I hope you will see this in
the same light in which it strikes me, and I
earnestly beg you to endeavour to settle it satis-
factorily on this ground ; for although nothing
can be more painful to me than to hesitate on
any point you think material, it would be in-
conceivably distressing to be urged on this subject. Indeed the great object of marking out
the leading supporters of Government is as well
or better obtained in the mode I propose than
the other ; and if you are enabled to offer the
Marquisates immediately, I think there can be
no difficulty in their relinquishing the other idea,
which was, as I have said, only a substitution ;
whereas you would now be enabled to gratify
them in their original object. I write in some
haste, and will add nothing on any other business at present, though, as I get a little leisure,
I shall trouble you on many other points. My
love to my brother, if he is still with you.—
Adieu, and believe me ever, most truly yours,
                                        W. Pitt.

P.S.—I rejoiced extremely in the opportunity of providing so well for Dr Ekins. Let me hope that it is some proof that I will not miss the occasion of accomplishing your wishes when I find it possible, and that you will believe whatever remains undone is not for want of inclination.

THE DUKE OF RUTLAND TO MR ORDE.

[*Most private.*]   BLACK ROCK, *July* 20, 1786.

MY DEAR SIR,—I write to you in a very great hurry, as you seem to press for an answer on some of the points contained in your letter of the 14th. On my receipt of your despatch of the 13th, I immediately returned you an answer, with an account of Lord Tyrone's and Lord Shannon's wishes in respect to their titles. You were perfectly correct as to both their ideas. Perhaps my letter came in time to add the name of Haverfordwest. I wrote likewise to Mr Pitt, in the most anxious terms, on the subject of their claims, which I hope has had its effect. As for the Englishmen who are recommended for Irish peerages, I confess it gives me much concern and embarrassment. I could most sincerely have wished that no step of that nature had taken effect, at least for a very long period.

It must, however, at all events, await the in-
tentions of my Government with respect to the
period of any creation at all, and those names
must be understood to be recommended subsequent to the claims of this country. The name
of Sir Sampson Gideon is what I must object
to. It will undoubtedly give offence in this
country, and a kind of offence which my aris-
tocratic pride recoils at finding my name to.
Another matter creates embarrassment; a Jew
of my own name (Jack Manners) applied to
me to recommend him as an Irish peer; I told
him that, having made a rule against the recommendation of Englishmen, I could not break
through it in any instance whatever. I must,
therefore, now write to him, to inform him
that this step is against my positive opinion
and representation, and of his Majesty's immediate nomination, without any origination
whatever from the Irish Government. I consent to the measure *in toto* with regret, but I
wish Sir Sampson could be excluded.

I am sorry our opinions differ on the business
of Lord Bellamont. With respect to the sale
of his pension, it is impossible for Government
to prevent his disposing of it if he can persuade
any one to become the purchaser, and I did
not think the favour of changing the name so
material as to refuse it to a man who now

seems disposed to be friendly. But, however, *l'affaire est finie;* so let it pass. I hope among those matters which must absolutely be settled forthwith, Sir Lucius will be considered one; my faith is personally pledged to him, and it must precede everything. With respect to Lord Mornington, if he can be satisfied by any English arrangement so much the better; but until that matter can be compassed his claim to the first Vice-Treasurership that may be given to Ireland must remain unimpeached. What becomes of the seat Jenkinson vacates? Will Lord Luttrell be now considered? If ever you meet or communicate with Lord Weymouth, pray assure him I will pay every attention to his recommendation of his agent. I could wish you, at some proper period, to mention to Mr Pitt my wish to recommend Major Hobart to his future patronage. He means to continue in Ireland no longer than the duration of my government. His views are English, and his political attachment I sincerely believe to be solely to me. He has views to a seat in Parliament, and in the event of his success I could hope that Mr Pitt would employ him in some respectable situation proper for his rank and his time of life. He has abilities, and I am sure will succeed when brought forward. This is a distant object, and therefore requires only to be stated to Mr Pitt; but if Mr Pitt should see him, he will much oblige me by mentioning to Major H. that I have not neglected his interest.

An extraordinary misapprehension has taken place respecting Major Dalrymple. I can assure you, that at no period did he ever mean to quit the army, to which he is enthusiastically attached. The transaction with Mr Vesey, if there be a secret history in it, is simply this: Capel Vesey wished to purchase a majority, and knowing my inclination to serve Major Dalrymple, and having no immediate means to get at my consent, as an inducement to me to agree to the purchase, held out to Dalrymple that he was willing to make an exchange with him for the majority of the 49th, about which he was negotiating. Military objections arising in the way of this business, it was dropped. Major Dalrymple had no desire to avoid going on service on any other ground than that of his debts. I beg this may be fairly stated as the whole secret of the business. Everything else that has been asserted also is false in fact, and false insinuation. I hope, therefore, nothing will be entertained to the prejudice of Major Dalrymple, who is a zealous, active, and spirited young officer.

The accounts from Munster have taken a more favourable turn, at least in the county of Limerick, if improper expectations were not held out to the deluded multitude. But I have not heard the precise particulars, only that a large proportion of these delinquents acknowledged their errors, and left their grievances to the redress of the Legislature. My intention is, if it be necessary, to give the command of the troops in that province, which amount now to pretty near two thousand, to Lord Luttrell, and that he may not absolutely depend on the timidity or negligence of country magistrates, to make him a privy councillor, by which he will be enabled to act entirely from himself. In a former period, Lord Drogheda was appointed for that sole reason, and the wisdom of it was proved. However, I hope the Legislature will in the next session take the grievances of the poor into their consideration, and, if possible, give them redress. The two great points which press are the tithes and the hearth-money. I desire you will turn them in your thoughts, and see if any effectual substitution occurs to you.

July 24.

The foregoing has been written a day or two, and was interrupted by my going for a day into the county of Wicklow, when I received a letter from Mr Pitt, to which I have returned the enclosed answer. If this matter fails, it is impossible I can remain in my Government with honour. I trust you will see this in the same light I do.—I am, &c.,   RUTLAND.

MR PITT TO THE DUKE OF RUTLAND.

[*Most secret.*]   DOWNING STREET, *Aug.* 19, 1786.

MY DEAR DUKE,—From the progress which has lately been made in settling the leading points of our commercial treaty with France, and from the negotiations depending both with Spain and Portugal, I am anxious to have, as early as possible, a full personal communication with those who are best enabled to discuss any point in which the interests of Ireland are involved. In the French treaty they are, perhaps, concerned to a less degree; but even in that I am in hopes that they may draw some benefit from the result; and at all events, I am anxious to hear whatever can be stated upon it before its conclusion. From *particular circumstances*, it seems of great consequence to bring this treaty *immediately* to a point. What I would therefore beg of you is, to prevail upon Mr Beresford and the Chancellor of the Exchequer, and, if possible, the Speaker, to come to England the first moment they can; if I might ask it, by *the return of the tide*. The leading principle of the treaty is, to put the subjects of the King's dominions and of France reciprocally on the terms on which the most favoured nation now stands (with a reserve for the Methuen treaty, in case Portugal makes it worth our while to agree to it); and secondly, to enumerate certain leading articles of manufacture which may be reciprocally imported at fixed duties. Our chief articles may probably be fixed at duties of from ten to twelve per cent. I mean by them the woollen, the cotton, hardware, and pottery; the French cambric at the same rate; their linens at the same duty as is now paid on other foreign linens (from which I am clear nothing can be feared, either to our manufactures or those of Ireland), and their wines and brandies at duties considerably reduced. It may be easily settled, that the rate to be fixed for linens shall not extend to Ireland, if she wishes not to allow its importation; and, indeed, as all the duties in the tariff are only to take place *reciprocally*, Ireland may waive (if it is thought proper) the whole of the tariff, and rest only on the terms of the most favoured nation. I conceive (as far as we can judge from our information) that Ireland may, on these terms, obtain a considerable trade in leather manufactures, in which our manufacturers apprehend Ireland to have an advantage.

And whatever is determined as to linens in
Ireland, many species of linen will, undoubtedly,
find their way through this country into France.

On the Portuguese and Spanish treaties I am
not yet prepared to state detail; but in the
former we shall certainly *insist* on Ireland's
having the full benefit of the Methuen treaty,
if *it is to be preserved at all.*

There is another point, which, if you concur
in what I have to suggest, will make the presence of the gentlemen I have mentioned particularly desirable. We are just going to give
a regular and permanent establishment to the
Committee of Council for the affairs of trade.
It is proposed, in enumerating the officers who
are to belong to it, to include in general terms
*any of the King's servants in Ireland who may
from time to time be members of the English
Privy Council.* This will, at all events, have a
conciliatory appearance. But what I should
wish, if you approve it, is to give it immediate
effect, by placing the Speaker, the Chancellor of
the Exchequer, the Secretary of State, and the
First Commissioner of the Revenue on the list
of the Privy Council; and the gentlemen to
whom I have alluded might be sworn immediately on their arrival. It would be a personal
compliment to them, and it would establish a
regular and easy communication, which might

be of material use on all questions of foreign
treaties and other commercial points which extend to both countries. As I apprehend you
may possibly be absent from Dublin, and there
is no time to lose, I have written another less
private letter, which I have desired Mr Hamilton
to open. — Believe me, my dear Duke, most
faithfully yours,   W. PITT.

MR PITT TO THE DUKE OF RUTLAND.

DOWNING STREET, *Aug.* 19, 1786.

MY DEAR LORD,—Some material points in the
treaties now depending with France and Spain,
and the discussion with Portugal, make me extremely anxious for some personal communication with those who can best state the interests
of Ireland as connected with these subjects.
From particular circumstances, part of this
question is become extremely pressing in point
of time. I would therefore beg of you, if you
approve it, to endeavour to prevail upon Mr
Beresford and the Chancellor of the Exchequer,
and if possible the Speaker, to come to London
the first moment they can. I am unwilling to
suggest troubling them so abruptly, but it is
material to the measures in agitation that our
consultation should be as speedy as possible.

L

There are also some other subjects which it may
be very advantageous to discuss at the same
time.   Let me only repeat that every hour may
be material.—I am, my dear Lord, your Grace's
most faithful and obedient servant,

W. PITT.

THE DUKE OF RUTLAND TO MR PITT.

BLACK ROCK, *September* 13, 1786.

MY DEAR PITT,—I should not have interrupted
you during your present important negotiations,
did not some matters which I wish to bring
under your consideration press exceedingly in
point of time for a decision.   In the first place,
I am to thank you for relieving me from the unpleasant predicament in which I should have
been constituted had not the engagement I had
respecting the two peerages been fulfilled.[1]   I
trust you will have no reason to repent of this
measure ; and in the censure which you suspected would be passed on the large creation,
and perhaps on some of the individuals who
composed it, I do not find the names of those
two noblemen to have been mingled in the
popular clamour.

---

[1] In August 1786 the Earls of Tyrone and Shannon were
created English Barons.

I understand Mr Orde is much recovered at Spa, so that I trust he will be able to resume his station in Ireland ; but he must determine on that measure speedily, as the affairs and the detail of this country will render his immediate return of absolute necessity. It is wise, however, to be prepared against every possible contingency, and in the event of his wishing to decline, let me ask, whom have you in your view to recommend competent to succeed him, remembering I can have no general objection to any one immediately connected with you ? But I should choose to be, for some time previous, apprised of the individual, because it may be possible personal reasons may render him, with every other essential qualification, not altogether the precise object of my election. Fitzherbert[1] you have long known to be my friend, and that I wished originally to have engaged him, but the distance and delicacy of his situation, and the pressure in point of time, rendered it then an impracticable measure or idea ; the same adverse reasons, I fear, may still remain. In a former letter you mentioned two other gentlemen, against whom we agreed no objections would lie ; but I wish to know whether you would now distinctly recommend either of them

[1] Alleyne Fitzherbert, in 1791 created Lord St Helen's in the Irish peerage.

to supply Orde's place.   If his health and spirits
oblige him to relinquish, a secretary must be
here by the beginning of the ensuing month.
Be so good, therefore, as to write to me very
fully on this matter, previous to any precise
determination, that I may be perfectly prepared
in case of any sudden new arrangement becoming necessary.

The accounts which have been received from
Lord Luttrell are as favourable as could have
been expected.   The counties through which he
has passed have in general been restored to a
state of tranquillity.   If any serious opposition
be made to the troops, it will arise in the county
of Kerry, whither he is proceeding.   The smug-
glers in that quarter are very numerous, and are
all in possession of arms, and it is reported they
threaten resistance, but this I much doubt.
Now I am speaking of Lord Luttrell, I cannot
avoid recommending him to your notice, which
I do with the utmost earnestness, as a man who
has been always zealous, and employed with
effect in the service of Government.   His object
is a regiment of dragoons, to which he has the
fairest pretensions from rank, independent of
any assistance he may derive from my influence
with you ; and I believe he claims a sort of promise from former Governments.   He has ever
been in the cavalry, and has declined a regiment

of infantry, in expectation of being promoted in the other line. General Cunningham has every claim but an absolute specific engagement to the *next* regiment of dragoons which may become vacant, but the expressions were so strong that it almost amounted to a promise; so he will, I trust, of course succeed on the first vacancy. But it would be a feather in my government, and of general service to the King's affairs, if, upon Lord Luttrell's return from Munster, I might be enabled to hold out to him the next succession to a regiment of dragoons (after General Cunningham's promotion) that may happen on this establishment. The service he has been employed upon is of a very delicate nature, and he has executed his commission with admirable address. But in truth the recommendation of the Lord Lieutenant should now and then be attended to in disposal of the regiments in this kingdom. I do not contend for the patronage of regiments, nor have I a wish to curtail the power of the Crown or the influence of English Government; but cases may arise, like the present, in which it may be wise to reward merit and exertion; and sometimes, indeed, the parliamentary necessities may require such an extension of the Lord Lieutenant's power of recommendation.

I understand from Mr Orde that you cannot

arrange the restoration of the Vice-Treasurers to Ireland. You must imagine it would be an object of great utility to his Majesty's Irish Government, both as a measure calculated to fasten on popularity, and at the same time as uniting the more solid advantage of creating new objects for ambition of the first men and the most extensive connections in this country. I do not, however, understand how entirely Lord Mornington has withdrawn his views from Ireland. While he continues to bend his eyes on Irish patronage, distinctly and unequivocally as that office, whenever it could be opened, has been pledged to him, I could not conceive myself justified in opening a treaty with any other individual till I have heard your explanation on the matter. This embarrassment should be precisely understood, whenever such an event shall take place or become necessary, as a judicious arrangement of this office might have the best influence on his Majesty's affairs, and greatly facilitate the measures of his Government. I strongly recommend the restoration of these offices, whenever you can render it practicable. I think the War Office might make an opening for Eden. I have always heard Sir G. Younge wished to be employed abroad in the diplomatic line; and if Fitzherbert were to be brought here, the arrangement might be accomplished at once.

The question of the tithes, with the commotions of the Whiteboys, will, I am apprehensive, form business for a very tedious session. A parliamentary investigation into the causes of their complaints will certainly take place, and is indeed become necessary. It is of the utmost consequence to prevent this question from falling into the hands of Opposition, who would employ it to the most mischievous purposes, and who might raise a storm which it would not be easy to direct. This business is of extreme delicacy and complication. We have the most rooted prejudices to contend with. The episcopal part of the clergy consider any settlement as a direct attack on their most ancient rights, and as a commencement of the ruin of their establishment ; whereas many individual clergymen, who foresee no prospect of receiving any property at all under the present system, are extremly desirous of a fair adjustment. The Established Church, with legions of Papists on one side, and a violent presbytery on the other, must be supported, however decidedly, as the principle that combinations are to compel measures must be exterminated out of the country and from the public mind ; at the same time, the country must not be permitted to continue in a state little less than war, when a substantial grievance is alleged to be the cause. The majority of the laity, who are at all times ready to oppose tithes, are likewise strong advocates for some settlement.   On the whole, it forms a most involved and difficult question ; on all hands it is agreed that it ought to be investigated, but then it is problematical whether any effectual remedy can be applied without endangering the Establishment, which must be guarded; and next, whether any arrangement could be suggested which the Church (who must be consulted) would agree to, adequate to the nature and extent of the evil complained of.   In short, it involves a great political settlement worthy of the decision of your clear and incomparable judgment.

I think I have now finished all I had to trouble you with which related to the public. You will next permit me to speak about my own private matters and applications.   Mr Orde informs me that, by my direction, he has brought them again under your consideration. Pulteney and Captain Molloy are *still* expectants, after repeated applications have been made in their favour of full two years' standing.   The finances of the first oblige me to make up the income of such an office as I have troubled you for to enable him to attend his duty in Parliament; and the other gentleman being married, and the term of the command of his ship being expired, he is extremely embarrassed, and I am equally anxious for his succession to something which may render him comfortable. I hope you will enable me to accomplish these arrangements before the meeting of Parliament. I am likewise requested by George Sutton to trouble you. I have assured him I will lay his situation before you ; but, as the possessor of a borough, I have recommended him to establish his claim in person. He has literally but £200 a-year to live upon. I think you might give him a pension of about £300, which would make him comfortable. A decayed gentleman, and particularly if a *member of Parliament*, is surely a proper object for such a provision. Mr Orde was likewise directed to mention to you the name of Major Hobart, who has views to a seat in Parliament, and who is introduced to your notice with the best wishes I can possibly give him. I have served him in this country, and have found him faithful, attached, with extreme good sense and judgment, and I am persuaded, brought properly forward, might be employed creditably to himself and usefully to Government. His objects in England are not immediate, and therefore cannot be precisely ascertained. All I have to request of you is to receive him, when he calls on you, as my friend, and express your favourable inclinations towards

him.   I must next come to the state of my parliamentary interest, which, since my departure
from England, I fear has been greatly in its
wane.   I will go at large into this without
making any apology, because as far as your
power (which stands indeed upon most substantial grounds) can be affected by any diminution of a parliamentary connection, you are
equally interested with myself.   With regard to
Scarborough, I must first premise, that the connection which my father formed there was solely
founded on the interest of Government, of which
he was permitted the exclusive patronage.   Be
assured every favour conceded to those who
have a claim upon Scarborough is a diminution
of my interest.   That interest is but an artificial one, nourished in the hotbed of Government favour, without any natural warmth;
while those who oppose me have an ancient
connection with the place, live in its vicinity,
and have those constant means of cultivating
a good intercourse with the inhabitants which
must ever of itself establish a member.   When
Mr Osbaldiston offered himself at the last election, his principles were supposed to be hostile
to your Government, which he was obliged
publicly to explain away previous to his being
elected.   This measure was forced upon him by
my friends on my account; and I can assure you

that the people of Scarborough entertain no idea
or wish to receive favours but through my intervention. As things have turned out, my interest is declining, and I trust I may not be
engaged in a disagreeable struggle which may
ultimately end in a defeat. If I cannot establish my exclusive claim to the patronage which
has usually gone to the inhabitants of that
place, I will concede all my future views on
it, and recommend to them to apply through
those other persons who, being on the spot,
have been generally more successful. I shall
thereby avoid the disgrace of being vanquished, and be no longer an importunate and
troublesome applicant to the Government to
which I am attached. I fear there has been
some mismanagement respecting the town of
Cambridge, and by the folly of Mortlake, whom
I wished to protect, I see a great difficulty in its
being rectified. You know the state of my interest in that county; it stands distinct from
every person; and Mortlake, who was one of my
most active instruments, involved himself, in
consequence of the support he gave me, with Mr
Yorke, who is my natural enemy there, who refused joining with me at the election, and who,
at a general meeting for the purpose, prevented
a statue from being erected to the memory of my
brother. Mr Yorke has certainly persecuted

him, and with the influence that he very naturally, and with justice, has with the present administration, has connected them in the persecu-
tion.   This has driven him into opposition, from
which I am anxious to recall him.   I wish you
would allow me to make his peace with Government, if it be possible.   Personally he weighs
not a feather; but he has decided influence in
the town of Cambridge, which I am apprehensive he will throw into the hands of the Duke of
Bedford, who is endeavouring to form a great
parliamentary strength, and with the hostility
of whose political inclinations you are well acquainted.   This will naturally introduce him
into the county, which must ultimately drive
me from all my views on both, and which I
have otherwise perpetually secured to my family.
You may remember I made a proposition to you
respecting the town of Cambridge before I quitted
England.   I have now laid before you all my
wants and my complaints, and, in short, everything connected with my private regards, my
personal weight and influence, and my public
situation, in the full confidence that they will
meet a favourable reception.—I am, &c.

RUTLAND.

MR PITT TO THE DUKE OF RUTLAND.

DOWNING STREET, *Oct.* 3, 1786.

MY DEAR DUKE,—You will easily excuse my writing you at this moment a very short letter, but I cannot delay acquainting you that the treaty of commerce was signed at Paris on the 26th ult. An official account shall soon be sent you, but in the meantime I enclose an abstract of all that is material. I am not quite without hopes the articles respecting linen may be so explained as to settle the duty for Ireland at the *hereditary duty* only, which I understand to be most for the interest of the Irish manufacture. We are trying at it, but as I cannot yet answer for it, nothing should yet be said of that hope. —Ever affectionately yours, W. PITT.

MR PITT TO THE DUKE OF RUTLAND.

[*Secret.*]   BURTON PYNSENT, *Nov.* 7, 1786.

MY DEAR DUKE,—I ought to have answered directly your inquiries respecting the duty on French wines, but Mr Fitzgibbon will have been able to satisfy you on that head. It is precisely as you imagined, that the duty in Ireland is to be *no more* than is now paid *there* on French wines. I have thought very much since I received your letter respecting the general state of Ireland, on the subjects suggested in that and your official letters to Lord Sydney. The question which arises is a nice and difficult one. On the one hand, the discontent seems general and rooted, and both that circumstance, and most of the accounts I hear, seem to indicate that there is some real grievance at bottom, which must be removed before any durable tranquillity can be secured. On the other hand, it is certainly a delicate thing to meddle with the Church Establishment in the present situation of Ireland; and anything like concession to the dangerous spirit which has shown itself is not without objection. But, on the whole, being persuaded that Government ought not to be afraid of incurring the imputation of weakness, by yielding in reasonable points, and can never make its stand effectually till it gets upon right ground, I think the great object ought to be, to ascertain fairly the true causes of complaint, to hold out a sincere disposition to give just redress, and a firm determination to do no more, taking care in the interval to hold up vigorously the execution of the law *as it stands* (till altered by Parliament), and to punish severely (if the means can be found) any tumultuous attempt

to violate it. I certainly think the institution
of tithe, especially if vigorously enforced, is
everywhere a great obstacle to the improvement and prosperity of any country. Many
circumstances in practice have made it less so
here : but even here it is felt; and there are
a variety of causes to make it sit much heavier
on Ireland. I believe, too, that it is as much
for the real interest of the Church as for that
of the land to adopt, if practicable, some other
mode of provision. If from any cause the
Church falls into general odium, Government
will be more likely to risk its own interests
than to save those of the Church by any efforts
in its favour. If, therefore, those who are at
the head of the clergy will look at it soberly
and dispassionately, they will see how incumbent it is upon them, in every point of view,
to propose some temperate accommodation ; and
even the appearance of concession, which might
be awkward in Government, could not be un-
becoming if it originated with them. The
thing to be aimed at, therefore, seems, as far
as I can judge of it, to find out a way of re-
moving the grievances arising out of a tithe,
or, perhaps, to substitute some new provision
in lieu of it ; to have such a plan cautiously
digested (which may require much time);
and, above all, to make the Church itself

the quarter to bring forward whatever is proposed.   How far this is practicable must depend
upon many circumstances, of which you can
form a nearer and better judgment, particularly
on the temper of the leading men among the
clergy.   I apprehend you may have a good deal
of difficulty with the Archbishop of Cashel;[1]
the Primate[2] is, I imagine, a man to listen to
temperate advice ; but it is surely desirable that
you should have as speedily as possible a full
communication with both of them ; and if you
feel the subject in the same light that I do, that,
while you state to them the full determination
of Government to give them all just and honourable support, you should impress them seriously
with the apprehension of their risking everything if they do not in time abandon ground
that is ultimately untenable.   To suggest the
precise plan of commutation which might be
adopted is more than I am equal to, and is premature ; but in general I have never seen any
good reason why a fair valuation should not be
made of the present amount of every living, and
a rent in corn to that amount be raised by a
pound rate on the several tenements in the

[1] Dr Charles Agar, afterwards translated to the Archbishopric
of Dublin.   In 1795 he was created Lord Somerton, and in 1806
Earl of Normanton.

[2] Dr Richard Robinson, Archbishop of Armagh.   He had been
in 1777 created Lord Rokeby.

parish, nearly according to the proportion in which they now contribute to tithe. When I say a rent in corn, I do not actually mean paid in corn, but a rent in money regulated by the average value from time to time of whatever number of bushels is at present equal to the fair value of the living. This would effectually prevent the Church from suffering by the fluctuations in the value of money, and it is a mode which was adopted in all college leases, in consequence, I believe, of an Act of Parliament in the time of Queen Elizabeth. I need not say that I throw out these ideas in personal confidence to yourself; and I shall wish much to know what you think of them, and whether you can make anything of your prelates, before any measure is officially suggested. It seems material that there should be the utmost secrecy till our line is decided upon, and it must be decided upon completely before Parliament meets.— Yours faithfully and sincerely, W. PITT.

P.S.—I return to town on Sunday or Monday next.

MR PITT TO THE DUKE OF RUTLAND.

[*Private.*]   DOWNING STREET,
                              Saturday Night, March 24, 1787.

MY DEAR DUKE,—From the circumstances
under which Lord Sydney's despatch arrived,
and your reasoning upon it, I am fully persuaded you could have pursued no other line
than you have done; at the same time there
would be a material inconvenience if no steps
are taken to prevent the ports of Ireland being
open to France on the terms of the treaty previous to opening those of France to Ireland and
Great Britain.   Lord Sydney's despatch will
state all that has occurred to us on the subject;
and we wish to be guided by your opinion on
the alternatives there stated.   I trust that postponing the return of the Bill till we receive your
answer can occasion you no trouble.   The only
point on which any alteration of any consequence
would in any event become necessary, is that
of the duty on *linens*, which is certainly very
important.   It stands in an embarrassed situation; but I do not despair of our bringing the
French Court to establish, on each side, the duty
you have enacted.   We have had no farther answer since you heard last, and there may be
some delay, as Mr Eden has been ill.   You shall

hear the moment we know anything new on the subject. If they do not agree entirely, it occurs to me, as a possible expedient, that it should be agreed to leave the duty on French linens coming to Ireland at a specific rate per ell, as it stands in your bill; but that the French should be at liberty, if they please, to lay 15 per cent, instead of the rate per ell, on Irish linens coming to France. Each of these duties will be conformable to Mr Eden's first declaration on the subject. The duty per ell in Ireland will answer the purposes of protecting the home market; and 15 per cent cannot, I should imagine, exclude your finest linens from a chance in the French market. At least I see no better solution. We will certainly not recur to this, unless the main object is unattainable; and I mention it now that you may consider of it beforehand, which will save time, if it should necessarily be brought into question. — Ever affectionately yours,   W. PITT.

THE DUKE OF RUTLAND TO MR PITT.

[*Private.*]   DUBLIN CASTLE, *April* 10, 1787.

MY DEAR PITT,—I find myself under extreme embarrassment respecting the motion which I understand is to be made to increase the estab-

lishment of the Prince of Wales. I had formerly, very unfortunately, and with too little
caution, involved myself upon this subject in a
manner which I fear I cannot in any shape or
under any notion of honour explain away or
recede from. I desired Lord Chatham to state
this circumstance to you when he was in Ireland
last year. I send you the papers which passed
between the Prince and myself on the accession
of the new ministry in 1782, by which you will
see how impossible it will be for me to take any
other line but that of supporting him, at least if
he calls on me for my support. I beg you will
let me hear from you immediately on this subject, as I shall depend upon you for explaining it
to the King, if I be necessitated to take a step
that may appear hostile to his Government, and
in opposition to his Majesty's private wishes, and
as such most extremely repugnant to my feelings
and principles.—I am, my dear Pitt, with unalterable regard, your affectionate friend,

RUTLAND.

MR PITT TO THE DUKE OF RUTLAND.

DOWNING STREET, *April* 14, 1787.

MY DEAR DUKE,—No exertion will be spared
on our part to prevail on the Court of France to

acquiesce in the duties on linens as settled in the
Irish Act ; but it is a work of so much difficulty
that we ought to be prepared for a contrary issue.
The duty of 4d. per ell was certainly stated in
Mr Eden's first declaration to amount to about
15 per cent on the average ; but if it turns out
to be much more than 15 per cent on linens of
such a price as those chiefly made in France, and
much less on those of such a price as are chiefly
made in Ireland, they seem to have too good
ground to say that this is contrary to the spirit
of the declaration. This depends upon the accu-
rate statement of the medium prices usually made
in each country. The best computations I have
seen make $4\frac{8}{20}$d. per ell 9 per cent nearly on the
average of Irish linens, and 18 per cent on
French. This on the face of it is not a fair reciprocity, and the admission of cambrics at a rate
supposed to be equal to about 12 per cent (for so
I understand it) in each country surely furnishes
no plea for such an inequality. As far as the
protection of the Irish market is concerned, surely
12 per cent, or less, is a full security against all
the world. To open the French market to Irish
linen at 9 per cent is more than can be fairly
contended for, and 12 per cent would give a
great advantage, and more than an equivalent
for the admission of cambric. At least Ireland
could not complain if the expedient were adopted

which I before stated,—that of leaving the duty
in Ireland as now fixed at 4d., and allowing the
French to impose, on their part, instead of 4d.,
12 per cent ad valorem. You would then be
completely safe at home, and have all you could
reasonably ask; nay, better terms than the declaration professed to obtain for Irish linens in
France. This is the way in which it strikes me,
but you are a better judge how it will be felt in
Ireland. What I most wish to press on your
consideration is, the dilemma to which you may
ultimately be driven. If our representations to
the French Court should fail of their full effect,
you must either find some expedient, or make
up your mind to renounce so much of the treaty
as relates to the fixed tariff. No efforts of ours
can prevent, in this case, the necessity of bringing the question again before your Parliament;
and you are to consider which will occasion least
dissatisfaction, to waive altogether the benefits
of this part of the treaty, or to admit a modifi-
cation consistent with the spirit of the whole
transaction, and seeming very much to come
under the meaning of that article which provides
for rectifying any mistakes which may from in-
advertence have found their way into the tariff.
You shall receive from time to time every information; but I beg you in the meantime to turn
this fully in your thoughts, as the difficulty is a

scrious one, and, notwithstanding all we can do, may become inevitable.—Ever sincerely yours,

W. PITT.

MR PITT TO THE DUKE OF RUTLAND.

DOWNING STREET,
Monday, April 29, 1787. One P.M.

MY DEAR DUKE,—I have great satisfaction in telling you that, by a despatch this instant received from Mr Eden, the French Government seem at length to have acquiesced entirely in the duties on linens as settled by the Irish Parliament. No formal consent seems yet to have been expressed, but there appears no doubt of the necessary orders being given to the French ports. For your more exact information I have desired the material part of Mr Eden's despatch to be immediately transmitted to you. This information, I hope, will be in time to save Mr Orde the trouble of his journey. Ever faithfully yours, W. PITT.

I anxiously hope to hear more favourable accounts of the Duchess's health.

P.S.—I conclude we shall hear in a few days from Mr Eden that the orders are actually given to the French ports. Though I have no doubt on the subject, it will perhaps be most prudent to defer announcing this publicly till such an account is actually received.   If any further explanation seems necessary respecting the breadth of the different sorts of linen, or any other particulars, be so good to send such observations as occur, as soon as the papers have been accurately examined.

THE DUKE OF RUTLAND TO MR PITT.

DUBLIN CASTLE, *May* 5, 1787.

MY DEAR PITT,—I need not describe to you the very unpleasant situation of my mind.   The King has not in his dominions a heart more warmly and zealously devoted to his person and to his service than mine; and under these impressions I find myself unequivocally pledged by an unqualified offer, made when I was very differently circumstanced, to support the proposal in Parliament for the arrangement of the Prince's affairs.   I rely entirely on your good offices to explain to the King the only bond (my word) which could fetter me in anything wherein his royal pleasure is concerned.   Could I prevail on myself, by any construction or mode of reasoning whatever, to depart from that word, I am convinced it would shake his Majesty's confidence in me, which I should consider as the greatest possible misfortune. The Prince has called on me to adhere to my engagement. He has reminded me of my solemn and voluntary pledge, and now claims its accomplishment. Contrary winds have delayed his messenger to the 3d instant, so that in all probability the business will be decided before my letters are received in London : they will, therefore, have no effect ; but I pretend to derive no merit from an accident which does not alter the nature though it changes the effect of my conduct. My sole motive is the solemn word by which I am pledged, and I am sanguine to hope this circumstance will not stamp an unfavourable impression on the King's mind ; and I shall look with an increased zeal to every opportunity of distinguishing the attachment and grateful duty which I most truly feel to my Sovereign.—I am, &c.,

RUTLAND.

MR PITT TO THE DUKE OF RUTLAND.

[*Secret.*]   DOWNING STREET, *Sept.* 17, 1787.

MY DEAR DUKE,—The affairs on the Continent which have long engaged our attention seem at length drawing to their crisis. The obstinacy of the party in Holland, in refusing satisfaction to

the King of Prussia, has probably before this
time compelled his army to act. Holland has
applied for the assistance of France, which she
seems determined to grant. If she does, the
assurances we have found it necessary to give,
both to Prussia and to the friends of the Stadt-
holder, as well as our uniform language to France
itself, will compel us to make preparations for
resisting her. This may draw on an immediate
war, which will, on every account, be abundantly
to be regretted; but the steps which have led
us so near to it could not, either with prudence
or credit, be avoided. I still think it possible,
from the infinite embarrassments of France, and
the little preparation she has yet made, that
things may stop short of actual extremity. An
appearance of vigour and firmness, accompanied
still, as I trust it has been throughout the discussion, with real moderation and temper, will
give us the best chance of this; but we must be
ready for the other alternative. You will not
wonder if, in these circumstances, I have not
leisure to write much on other subjects. Let
me, however, acknowledge your letter relative to
the provision for Mrs Orde, which, under the circumstances you mention, is perfectly unexceptionable. It seems to me clear he can never
return to the fatigues of his situation, and we
should at least be prepared as to his successor.

Fitzherbert is quitting Russia, on account of his health, and will be here soon. If you continue to wish it, perhaps he would do better than any one else. The Bishop of Ferns[1] mentioned to me your plan about the town of Cambridge, which I must write about more at large, and which I will certainly do *whatever I can* to promote. As to other points to which you refer, I wish to know them more particularly; but I am sure you do me injustice if you think me disposed to be either indifferent or inattentive to your interests or wishes when I have the means of promoting them.—Believe me ever sincerely and faithfully yours, W. PITT.

MR PITT TO THE DUKE OF RUTLAND.

[*Secret.*]   DOWNING STREET,
                    Wednesday Night, Sept. 26, 1787.

MY DEAR DUKE,—The complexion of affairs is not yet decided, though the success in Holland makes our prospect in any event a good one, and I trust makes peace the most probable. The result of the instructions sent by Mr Grenville to Paris, and the further accounts from the Hague, especially of what may pass at Amsterdam, will soon enable us to judge what may be expected. In the meantime, I am sure you will agree with

---

[1] Dr William Preston.

me that every moment is precious, and that we cannot be too vigorous or universal in our preparations. I am sure, therefore, you will use every exertion, in consequence of the despatch you will receive by this messenger from Lord Sydney. Nothing can be more reasonable than that the regiments which Ireland furnishes for foreign service should be immediately completed to the augmented establishment. There seems no way of doing this without delay but by drafts from the regiments in Ireland, and these may be replaced by recruiting (with the aid of the war bounty) long before Ireland can have anything to apprehend from abroad. As to the state of the country within, I do not imagine the temporary loss of 1500 men can produce any inconvenience, followed, as it will be, by recruiting immediately, to replace that number, and, whenever it is necessary, by augmenting all the regiments in Ireland, as we are doing here. You will probably think it right to let the friends of Government in every part of the country understand, that immediate efforts are necessary for the general interests of the empire, but that measures will be taken at the same time for their complete security at home. Perhaps the idea of proposing next session a Militia Bill (if one can be properly digested) may be of use, to prevent any attempt towards reviving the volunteers. At all events, you will feel, I am persuaded, that no local or temporary difficulties ought to stand in the way of vigorous exertions at a crisis in which early preparation may decide so much on the future state of this country, in case either of war or negotiation. With the fullest confidence in your sentiments on such an occasion, I have only to recommend this subject to your most immediate attention. *Not a moment ought to be lost.* All our provisional measures for operations may depend, in a great degree, upon it. — Ever affectionately yours, W. PITT.

P.S.—I think the Irish Parliament will not make any difficulty about expense on such an occasion ; but if we get the troops (which is our first object), we shall make no difficulty in settling the accounts.[1]

[1] The Duke of Rutland died on the 24th of October following. He was only thirty-three years of age.

THE END.

PRINTED BY WILLIAM BLACKWOOD AND SONS.

67. Tithes.

CATALOGUE

OF

MESSRS BLACKWOOD & SONS'

PUBLICATIONS.

CATALOGUE

OF

MESSRS BLACKWOOD & SONS

PUBLICATIONS.

———◆———

ALISON. History of Europe. By Sir ARCHIBALD ALISON, Bart.,
D.C.L.

1. From the Commencement of the French Revolution to the
Battle of Waterloo.
   LIBRARY EDITION, 14 vols., with Portraits. Demy 8vo, £10, 10s.
   ANOTHER EDITION, in 20 vols. crown 8vo, £6.
   PEOPLE'S EDITION, 13 vols. crown 8vo, £2, 11s.

2. Continuation to the Accession of Louis Napoleon.
   LIBRARY EDITION, 8 vols. 8vo, £6, 7s. 6d.
   PEOPLE'S EDITION, 8 vols. crown 8vo, 34s.

3. Epitome of Alison's History of Europe. Twenty-ninth
Thousand, 7s. 6d.

4. Atlas to Alison's History of Europe. By A. Keith Johnston.
   LIBRARY EDITION, demy 4to, £3, 3s.
   PEOPLE'S EDITION, 31s. 6d.

——— Life of John Duke of Marlborough. With some Account
of his Contemporaries, and of the War of the Succession. Third Edition,
2 vols. 8vo. Portraits and Maps, 30s.

——— Essays: Historical, Political, and Miscellaneous. 3 vols.
demy 8vo, 45s.

ACTA SANCTORUM HIBERNIÆ; Ex Codice Salmanticensi.
Nunc primum integre edita opera CAROLI DE SMEDT et JOSEPHI DE BACKER,
e Soc. Jesu, Hagiographorum Bollandianorum; Auctore et Sumptus Largiente
JOANNE PATRICIO MARCHIONE BOTHAE. In One handsome 4to Volume, bound
in half roxburghe, £2, 2s.; in paper wrapper, 31s. 6d.

AIRD. Poetical Works of Thomas Aird. Fifth Edition, with
Memoir of the Author by the Rev. JARDINE WALLACE, and Portrait.
Crown 8vo, 7s. 6d.

ALLARDYCE. The City of Sunshine. By ALEXANDER ALLAR-
DYCE. Three vols. post 8vo, £1, 5s. 6d.

——— Memoir of the Honourable George Keith Elphinstone,
K.B., Viscount Keith of Stonehaven, Marischal, Admiral of the Red. 8vo,
with Portrait, Illustrations, and Maps, 21s.

ALMOND. Sermons by a Lay Head-master. By HELY HUTCHIN-
SON ALMOND, M.A. Oxon., Head-master of Loretto School. Crown 8vo, 5s.

ANCIENT CLASSICS FOR ENGLISH READERS. Edited by Rev. W. LUCAS COLLINS, M.A. Price 2s. 6d. each. *For list of Volumes, see* page 2.

AYTOUN. Lays of the Scottish Cavaliers, and other Poems. By W. EDMONDSTOUNE AYTOUN, D.C.L., Professor of Rhetoric and Belles-Lettres in the University of Edinburgh. New Edition, printed from a new type, and tastefully bound. Fcap. 8vo, 3s. 6d.
Another Edition, being the Thirtieth. Fcap. 8vo, cloth extra, 7s. 6d.
Cheap Edition. Fcap. 8vo. Illustrated Cover. Price 1s.
—— An Illustrated Edition of the Lays of the Scottish Cavaliers. From designs by Sir NOEL PATON. Small 4to, in gilt cloth, 21s.
—— Bothwell : a Poem. Third Edition. Fcap., 7s. 6d.
—— Poems and Ballads of Goethe. Translated by Professor AYTOUN and Sir THEODORE MARTIN, K.C.B. Third Edition. Fcap., 6s.
—— Bon Gaultier's Book of Ballads. By the SAME. Fifteenth and Cheaper Edition. With Illustrations by Doyle, Leech, and Crowquill. Fcap. 8vo, 5s.
—— The Ballads of Scotland. Edited by Professor AYTOUN. Fourth Edition. 2 vols. fcap. 8vo, 12s.
—— Memoir of William E. Aytoun, D.C.L. By Sir THEODORE MARTIN, K.C.B. With Portrait. Post 8vo, 12s.

BACH. On Musical Education and Vocal Culture. By ALBERT B. BACH. Fourth Edition. 8vo, 7s. 6d.
—— The Principles of Singing. A Practical Guide for Vocalists and Teachers. With Course of Vocal Exercises. Crown 8vo, 6s.
—— The Art of Singing. With Musical Exercises for Young People. Crown 8vo, 3s.

BALLADS AND POEMS. By MEMBERS OF THE GLASGOW BALLAD CLUB. Crown 8vo, 7s. 6d

BANNATYNE. Handbook of Republican Institutions in the United States of America. Based upon Federal and State Laws, and other reliable sources of information. By DUGALD J. BANNATYNE, Scotch Solicitor, New York ; Member of the Faculty of Procurators, Glasgow. Cr. 8vo, 7s. 6d.

BELLAIRS. The Transvaal War, 1880-81. Edited by Lady BELLAIRS. With a Frontispiece and Map. 8vo, 15s.
—— Gossips with Girls and Maidens, Betrothed and Free. New Edition. Crown 8vo, 5s.

BESANT. The Revolt of Man. By WALTER BESANT, M.A. Eighth Edition. Crown 8vo, 3s. 6d.
—— Readings in Rabelais. Crown 8vo, 7s. 6d.

BEVERIDGE. Culross and Tulliallan; or Perthshire on Forth. Its History and Antiquities. With Elucidations of Scottish Life and Character from the Burgh and Kirk-Session Records of that District. By DAVID BEVERIDGE. 2 vols. 8vo, with Illustrations, 42s.
—— Between the Ochils and the Forth ; or, From Stirling Bridge to Aberdour. Crown 8vo, 6s.

BLACK. Heligoland and the Islands of the North Sea. By WILLIAM GEORGE BLACK. Crown 8vo, 4s.

BLACKIE. Lays and Legends of Ancient Greece. By JOHN STUART BLACKIE, Emeritus Professor of Greek in the University of Edinburgh. Second Edition. Fcap. 8vo. 5s.
—— The Wisdom of Goethe. Fcap. 8vo. Cloth, extra gilt, 6s.
—— Scottish Song : Its Wealth, Wisdom, and Social Significance. Crown 8vo. With Music. 7s. 6d.
—— A Song of Heroes. Crown 8vo, 6s.

BLACKWOOD'S MAGAZINE, from Commencement in 1817 to October 1889. Nos. 1 to 888, forming 144 Volumes.
—— Index to Blackwood's Magazine. Vols. 1 to 50. 8vo, 15s.

BLACKWOOD. Tales from Blackwood. Forming Twelve Volumes of Interesting and Amusing Railway Reading. Price One Shilling each, in Paper Cover. Sold separately at all Railway Bookstalls.
They may also be had bound in cloth, 18s., and in half calf, richly gilt, 30s.
Or 12 volumes in 6, roxburghe, 21s., and half red morocco, 28s.

——— Tales from Blackwood. New Series. Complete in Twenty-four Shilling Parts. Handsomely bound in 12 vols., cloth, 30s. In leather back, roxburghe style, 37s. 6d. In half calf, gilt, 52s. 6d. In half morocco, 55s.
In course of Publication.

——— Tales from Blackwood. Third Series. In Parts. Each price 1s. [*Nos. I. to VI. now ready.*
In course of Publication.

——— Travel, Adventure, and Sport. From 'Blackwood's Magazine.' In Parts. Uniform with 'Tales from Blackwood.' Each price 1s. [*Nos. I. to V. now ready.*

——— Standard Novels. Uniform in size and legibly Printed. Each Novel complete in one volume.
FLORIN SERIES, Illustrated Boards. Or in New Cloth Binding, 2s. 6d.

TOM CRINGLE'S LOG. By Michael Scott.	PEN OWEN. By Dean Hook.
THE CRUISE OF THE MIDGE. By the Same.	ADAM BLAIR. By J. G. Lockhart.
CYRIL THORNTON. By Captain Hamilton.	LADY LEE'S WIDOWHOOD. By General
ANNALS OF THE PARISH. By John Galt.	Sir E. B. Hamley.
THE PROVOST, &c. By John Galt.	SALEM CHAPEL. By Mrs Oliphant.
SIR ANDREW WYLIE. By John Galt.	THE PERPETUAL CURATE. By Mrs Oli-
THE ENTAIL. By John Galt.	phant.
MISS MOLLY. By Beatrice May Butt.	MISS MARJORIBANKS. By Mrs Oliphant.
REGINALD DALTON. By J. G. Lockhart.	JOHN : A Love Story. By Mrs Oliphant.

SHILLING SERIES, Illustrated Cover. Or in New Cloth Binding, 1s. 6d.

THE RECTOR, and THE DOCTOR'S FAMILY. By Mrs Oliphant.	SIR FRIZZLE PUMPKIN, NIGHTS AT MESS, &c.
THE LIFE OF MANSIE WAUCH. By D. M. Moir.	THE SUBALTERN.
	LIFE IN THE FAR WEST. By G. F. Ruxton.
PENINSULAR SCENES AND SKETCHES. By F. Hardman.	VALERIUS : A Roman Story. By J. G. Lockhart.

BLACKMORE. The Maid of Sker. By R. D. BLACKMORE, Author of 'Lorna Doone,' &c. New Edition. Crown 8vo, 6s.

BLAIR. History of the Catholic Church of Scotland. From the Introduction of Christianity to the Present Day. By ALPHONS BELLESHEIM, D.D., Canon of Aix-la-Chapelle. Translated, with Notes and Additions, by D. OSWALD HUNTER BLAIR, O.S.B., Monk of Fort Augustus. To be completed in 4 vols. 8vo. Vols. I. and II. 25s. Vol. III. 12s. 6d.

BOSCOBEL TRACTS. Relating to the Escape of Charles the Second after the Battle of Worcester, and his subsequent Adventures. Edited by J. HUGHES, Esq., A.M. A New Edition, with additional Notes and Illustrations, including Communications from the Rev. R. H. BARHAM, Author of the 'Ingoldsby Legends.' 8vo, with Engravings, 16s.

BROOKE, Life of Sir James, Rajah of Sarāwak. From his Personal Papers and Correspondence. By SPENSER ST JOHN, H.M.'s Minister-Resident and Consul-General Peruvian Republic ; formerly Secretary to the Rajah. With Portrait and a Map. Post 8vo, 12s. 6d.

BROUGHAM. Memoirs of the Life and Times of Henry Lord Brougham. Written by HIMSELF. 3 vols. 8vo, £2, 8s. The Volumes are sold separately, price 16s. each.

BROWN. The Forester : A Practical Treatise on the Planting, Rearing, and General Management of Forest-trees. By JAMES BROWN, LL.D., Inspector of and Reporter on Woods and Forests. Fifth Edition, revised and enlarged. Royal 8vo, with Engravings, 36s.

BROWN. The Ethics of George Eliot's Works. By JOHN CROMBIE BROWN. Fourth Edition. Crown 8vo, 2s. 6d.

BRYDALL. Art in Scotland ; its Origin and Progress. By ROBERT BRYDALL, Master of St George's Art School of Glasgow. 8vo, 12s. 6d.

BROWN. A Manual of Botany, Anatomical and Physiological.
For the Use of Students. By ROBERT BROWN, M.A., Ph.D. Crown 8vo, with
numerous Illustrations, 12s. 6d.

BRUCE. In Clover and Heather. Poems by WALLACE BRUCE.
Crown 8vo, 4s. 6d.
A limited number of Copies on large hand-made paper.

BUCHAN. Introductory Text-Book of Meteorology. By ALEX-
ANDER BUCHAN, M.A., F.R.S.E., Secretary of the Scottish Meteorological
Society, &c. Crown 8vo, with 8 Coloured Charts and Engravings, 4s. 6d.

BUCHANAN. The Shire Highlands (East Central Africa). By
JOHN BUCHANAN, Planter at Zomba. Crown 8vo, 5s.

BURBIDGE. Domestic Floriculture, Window Gardening, and
Floral Decorations. Being practical directions for the Propagation, Culture,
and Arrangement of Plants and Flowers as Domestic Ornaments. By F. W.
BURBIDGE. Second Edition. Crown 8vo, with numerous Illustrations, 7s. 6d.

—————— Cultivated Plants : Their Propagation and Improvement.
Including Natural and Artificial Hybridisation, Raising from Seed, Cuttings,
and Layers, Grafting and Budding, as applied to the Families and Genera in
Cultivation. Crown 8vo, with numerous Illustrations, 12s. 6d.

BURTON. The History of Scotland : From Agricola's Invasion to
the Extinction of the last Jacobite Insurrection. By JOHN HILL BURTON,
D.C.L., Historiographer-Royal for Scotland. New and Enlarged Edition.
8 vols., and Index. Crown 8vo, £3, 3s.

—————— History of the British Empire during the Reign of Queen
Anne. In 3 vols. 8vo. 36s.

—————— The Scot Abroad. Third Edition. Crown 8vo, 10s. 6d.

—————— The Book-Hunter. New Edition. With Portrait. Crown
8vo, 7s. 6d.

BUTE. The Roman Breviary : Reformed by Order of the Holy
Œcumenical Council of Trent ; Published by Order of Pope St Pius V.; and
Revised by Clement VIII. and Urban VIII.; together with the Offices since
granted. Translated out of Latin into English by JOHN, Marquess of Bute,
K.T. In 2 vols, crown 8vo. cloth boards, edges uncut. £2, 2s.

—————— The Altus of St Columba. With a Prose Paraphrase and
Notes. In paper cover, 2s. 6d.

BUTLER. Pompeii : Descriptive and Picturesque. By W.
BUTLER. Post 8vo, 5s.

BUTT. Miss Molly. By BEATRICE MAY BUTT. Cheap Edition, 2s.

—————— Eugenie. Crown 8vo, 6s. 6d.

—————— Elizabeth, and Other Sketches. Crown 8vo, 6s.

—————— Novels. New and Uniform Edition. Crown 8vo, each 2s. 6d.
Delicia. *Now ready.*

CAIRD. Sermons. By JOHN CAIRD, D.D., Principal of the University of Glasgow. Sixteenth Thousand. Fcap. 8vo, 5s.

—————— Religion in Common Life. A Sermon preached in Crathie
Church, October 14, 1855, before Her Majesty the Queen and Prince Albert.
Published by Her Majesty's Command. Cheap Edition, 3d.

CAMPBELL. Sermons Preached before the Queen at Balmoral.
By the Rev. A. A. CAMPBELL, Minister of Crathie. Published by Command
of Her Majesty. Crown 8vo, 4s. 6d.

CAMPBELL. Records of Argyll. Legends, Traditions, and Recollections of Argyllshire Highlanders, collected chiefly from the Gaelic.
With Notes on the Antiquity of the Dress, Clan Colours or Tartans of the
Highlanders. By LORD ARCHIBALD CAMPBELL. Illustrated with Nineteen
full-page Etchings. 4to, printed on hand-made paper, £3, 3s.

CANTON. A Lost Epic, and other Poems. By WILLIAM CANTON.
Crown 8vo, 5s.

CARR. Margaret Maliphant. A Novel. By Mrs COMYNS CARR,
Author of 'La Fortunina,' ' North Italian Folk,' &c. 3 vols. post 8vo, 25s. 6d.

CARRICK. Koumiss; or, Fermented Mare's Milk: and its Uses
in the Treatment and Cure of Pulmonary Consumption, and other Wasting
Diseases. With an Appendix on the best Methods of Fermenting Cow's Milk.
By GEORGE L. CARRICK, M.D., L.R.C.S.E. and L.R.C.P.E., Physician to the
British Embassy, St Petersburg, &c. Crown 8vo, 10s. 6d.

CAUVIN. A Treasury of the English and German Languages.
Compiled from the best Authors and Lexicographers in both Languages.
By JOSEPH CAUVIN, LL.D. and Ph.D., of the University of Göttingen, &c.
Crown 8vo, 7s. 6d.

CAVE-BROWN. Lambeth Palace and its Associations. By J.
CAVE-BROWN, M.A., Vicar of Detling, Kent, and for many years Curate of Lam-
beth Parish Church. With an Introduction by the Archbishop of Canterbury.
Second Edition, containing an additional Chapter on Medieval Life in the
Old Palaces. 8vo, with Illustrations, 21s.

CHARTERIS. Canonicity; or, Early Testimonies to the Existence
and Use of the Books of the New Testament. Based on Kirchhoffer's 'Quel-
lensammlung.' Edited by A. H. CHARTERIS, D.D., Professor of Biblical
Criticism in the University of Edinburgh. 8vo, 18s.

CHRISTISON. Life of Sir Robert Christison, Bart., M.D., D.C.L.
Oxon., Professor of Medical Jurisprudence in the University of Edinburgh.
Edited by his SONS. In two vols. 8vo. Vol I.—Autobiography. 16s. Vol. II.
—Memoirs. 16s.

CHURCH SERVICE SOCIETY. A Book of Common Order:
Being Forms of Worship issued by the Church Service Society. Fifth Edition. 6s.

CLELAND. Barbara Allan, the Provost's Daughter. By ROBERT
CLELAND, Author of 'Inchbracken,' 'True to a Type,' &c. 2 vols., 17s.

CLOUSTON. Popular Tales and Fictions: their Migrations and
Transformations. By W. A. CLOUSTON, Editor of 'Arabian Poetry for English Readers,' 'The Book of Sindibad,' &c. 2 vols. post 8vo, roxburghe binding. 25s.

COBBAN. Master of his Fate. By J. MACLAREN COBBAN, Author
of 'The Cure of Souls,' 'Tinted Vapours,' &c. Crown 8vo, 3s. 6d.

COCHRAN. A Handy Text-Book of Military Law. Compiled
chiefly to assist Officers preparing for Examination; also for all Officers of
the Regular and Auxiliary Forces. Comprising also a Synopsis of part of
the Army Act. By Major F. COCHRAN, Hampshire Regiment Garrison In-
structor, North British District. Crown 8vo, 7s. 6d.

COLQUHOUN. The Moor and the Loch. Containing Minute
Instructions in all Highland Sports, with Wanderings over Crag and Corrie,
Flood and Fell. By JOHN COLQUHOUN. Seventh Edition. With Illustra-
tions. 8vo, 21s.

COTTERILL. Suggested Reforms in Public Schools. By C. C.
COTTERILL, M.A., Assistant Master at Fettes College, Edin. Crown 8vo, 3s. 6d.

CRANSTOUN. The Elegies of Albius Tibullus. Translated into
. English Verse, with Life of the Poet, and Illustrative Notes. By JAMES CRAN-
STOUN, LL.D., Author of a Translation of 'Catullus.' Crown 8vo, 6s. 6d.

—— The Elegies of Sextus Propertius. Translated into English
Verse, with Life of the Poet, and Illustrative Notes. Crown 8vo, 7s. 6d.

CRAWFORD. Saracinesca. By F. MARION CRAWFORD, Author of
'Mr Isaacs,' 'Dr Claudius,' 'Zoroaster.' &c. &c. Fourth Ed. Crown 8vo, 6s.

CRAWFORD. The Doctrine of Holy Scripture respecting the
Atonement. By the late THOMAS J. CRAWFORD, D.D., Professor of Divinity in
the University of Edinburgh. Fifth Edition. 8vo, 12s.

—— The Fatherhood of God, Considered in its General
and Special Aspects, and particularly in relation to the Atonement, with a
Review of Recent Speculations on the Subject. By the late THOMAS J.
CRAWFORD, D.D., Professor of Divinity in the University of Edinburgh.
Third Edition, Revised and Enlarged. 8vo, 9s.

—— The Preaching of the Cross, and other Sermons. 8vo, 7s. 6d.

—— The Mysteries of Christianity. Crown 8vo, 7s. 6d.

CRAWFORD. An Atonement of East London, and other Poems. By HOWARD CRAWFORD, M.A. Crown 8vo, 5s.

DAVIES. Norfolk Broads and Rivers; or, The Waterways, Lagoons, and Decoys of East Anglia. By G. CHRISTOPHER DAVIES, Author of 'The Swan and her Crew.' Illustrated with Seven full-page Plates. New and Cheaper Edition. Crown 8vo, 6s.

—— Our Home in Aveyron. Sketches of Peasant Life in Aveyron and the Lot. By G. CHRISTOPHER DAVIES and Mrs BROUGHALL. Illustrated with full-page Illustrations. In 1 vol. 8vo, 15s.

DAYNE. In the Name of the Tzar. A Novel. By J. BELFORD DAYNE. Crown 8vo, 6s.

—— Tribute to Satan. A Novel. Crown 8vo, 2s. 6d.

DE LA WARR. An Eastern Cruise in the 'Edeline.' By the Countess DE LA WARR. In Illustrated Cover. 2s.

DESCARTES. The Method, Meditations, and Principles of Philosophy of Descartes. Translated from the Original French and Latin. With a New Introductory Essay, Historical and Critical, on the Cartesian Philosophy. By JOHN VEITCH, LL.D., Professor of Logic and Rhetoric in the University of Glasgow. A New Edition, being the Ninth. Price 6s. 6d.

DICKSON. Gleanings from Japan. By W. G. DICKSON, Author of 'Japan: Being a Sketch of its History, Government, and Officers of the Empire.' With Illustrations. 8vo, 16s.

DOGS, OUR DOMESTICATED: Their Treatment in reference to Food, Diseases, Habits, Punishment, Accomplishments. By 'MAGENTA.' Crown 8vo, 2s. 6d.

DR HERMIONE. By the Author of 'Lady Bluebeard,' 'Zit and Xoe.' In 1 vol., crown 8vo, 6s.

DU CANE. The Odyssey of Homer, Books I.-XII. Translated into English Verse. By Sir CHARLES DU CANE, K.C.M.G. 8vo, 10s. 6d.

DUDGEON. History of the Edinburgh or Queen's Regiment Light Infantry Militia, now 3rd Battalion The Royal Scots; with an Account of the Origin and Progress of the Militia, and a Brief Sketch of the old Royal Scots. By Major R. C. DUDGEON, Adjutant 3rd Battalion The Royal Scots. Post 8vo, with Illustrations. 10s. 6d.

DUNCAN. Manual of the General Acts of Parliament relating to the Salmon Fisheries of Scotland from 1828 to 1882. By J. BARKER DUNCAN. Crown 8vo, 5s.

DUNSMORE. Manual of the Law of Scotland as to the Relations between Agricultural Tenants and their Landlords, Servants, Merchants, and Bowers. By W. DUNSMORE. Crown 8vo, 7s. 6d.

DUPRÈ. Thoughts on Art, and Autobiographical Memoirs of Giovanni Duprè. Translated from the Italian by E. M. PERUZZI, with the permission of the Author. New Edition. With an Introduction by W. W. STORY. Crown 8vo, 10s. 6d.

ELIOT. George Eliot's Life, Related in her Letters and Journals. Arranged and Edited by her husband, J. W. CROSS. With Portrait and other Illustrations. Third Edition. 3 vols. post 8vo, 42s.

—— Works of George Eliot (Cabinet Edition). Handsomely printed in a new type, 21 volumes, crown 8vo, price £5, 5s. The Volumes are also sold separately, price 5s. each, viz.:—

> Romola. 2 vols.—Silas Marner, The Lifted Veil, Brother Jacob. 1 vol.— Adam Bede. 2 vols.—Scenes of Clerical Life. 2 vols.—The Mill on the Floss. 2 vols.—Felix Holt. 2 vols.—Middlemarch. 3 vols.— Daniel Deronda. 3 vols.—The Spanish Gypsy. 1 vol.—Jubal, and other Poems, Old and New. 1 vol.—Theophrastus Such. 1 vol.— Essays. 1 vol.

—— George Eliot's Life. (Cabinet Edition.) With Portrait and other Illustrations. 3 vols. crown 8vo, 15s.

—— George Eliot's Life. With Portrait and other Illustrations. New Edition, in one volume. Crown 8vo, 7s. 6d.

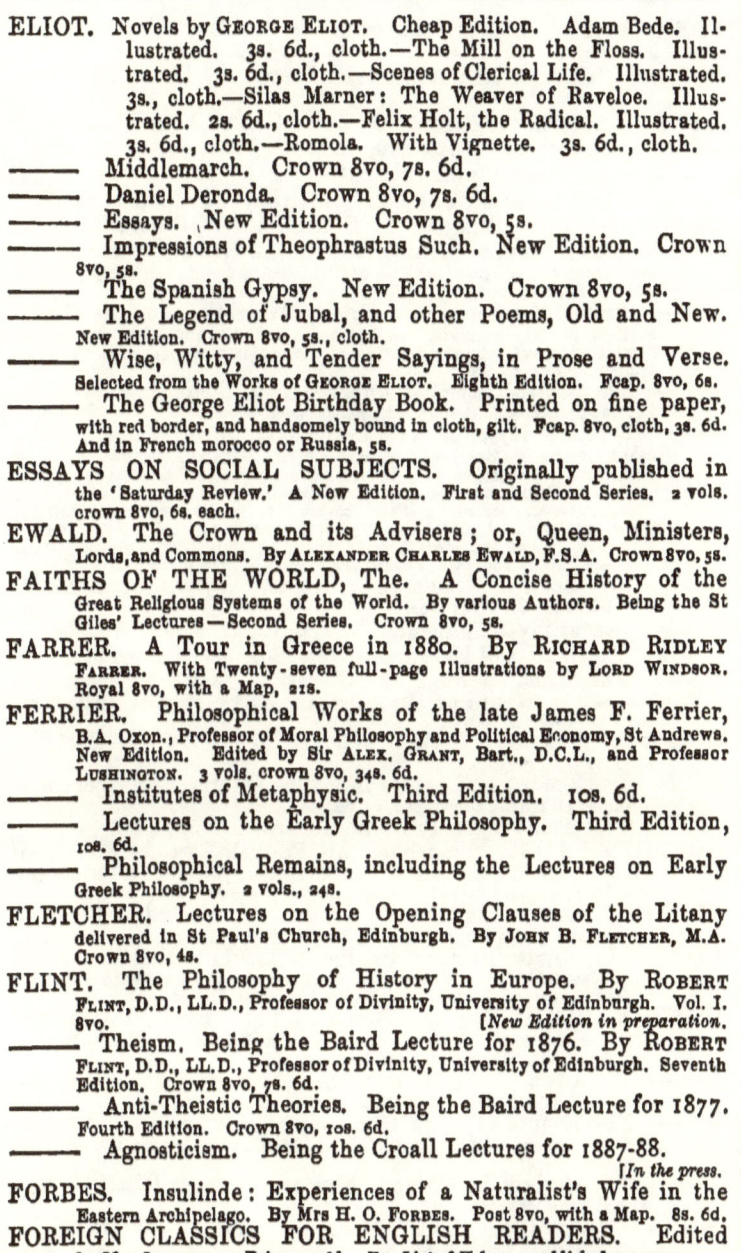

ELIOT. Novels by GEORGE ELIOT. Cheap Edition. Adam Bede. Illustrated. 3s. 6d., cloth.—The Mill on the Floss. Illustrated. 3s. 6d., cloth.—Scenes of Clerical Life. Illustrated. 3s., cloth.—Silas Marner: The Weaver of Raveloe. Illustrated. 2s. 6d., cloth.—Felix Holt, the Radical. Illustrated. 3s. 6d., cloth.—Romola. With Vignette. 3s. 6d., cloth.

—— Middlemarch. Crown 8vo, 7s. 6d.

—— Daniel Deronda. Crown 8vo, 7s. 6d.

—— Essays. New Edition. Crown 8vo, 5s.

—— Impressions of Theophrastus Such. New Edition. Crown 8vo, 5s.

—— The Spanish Gypsy. New Edition. Crown 8vo, 5s.

—— The Legend of Jubal, and other Poems, Old and New. New Edition. Crown 8vo, 5s., cloth.

—— Wise, Witty, and Tender Sayings, in Prose and Verse. Selected from the Works of GEORGE ELIOT. Eighth Edition. Fcap. 8vo, 6s.

—— The George Eliot Birthday Book. Printed on fine paper, with red border, and handsomely bound in cloth, gilt. Fcap. 8vo, cloth, 3s. 6d. And in French morocco or Russia, 5s.

ESSAYS ON SOCIAL SUBJECTS. Originally published in the 'Saturday Review.' A New Edition. First and Second Series. 2 vols. crown 8vo, 6s. each.

EWALD. The Crown and its Advisers; or, Queen, Ministers, Lords, and Commons. By ALEXANDER CHARLES EWALD, F.S.A. Crown 8vo, 5s.

FAITHS OF THE WORLD, The. A Concise History of the Great Religious Systems of the World. By various Authors. Being the St Giles' Lectures—Second Series. Crown 8vo, 5s.

FARRER. A Tour in Greece in 1880. By RICHARD RIDLEY FARRER. With Twenty-seven full-page Illustrations by LORD WINDSOR. Royal 8vo, with a Map, 21s.

FERRIER. Philosophical Works of the late James F. Ferrier, B.A. Oxon., Professor of Moral Philosophy and Political Economy, St Andrews. New Edition. Edited by Sir ALEX. GRANT, Bart., D.C.L., and Professor LUSHINGTON. 3 vols. crown 8vo, 34s. 6d.

—— Institutes of Metaphysic. Third Edition. 10s. 6d.

—— Lectures on the Early Greek Philosophy. Third Edition, 10s. 6d.

—— Philosophical Remains, including the Lectures on Early Greek Philosophy. 2 vols., 24s.

FLETCHER. Lectures on the Opening Clauses of the Litany delivered in St Paul's Church, Edinburgh. By JOHN B. FLETCHER, M.A. Crown 8vo, 4s.

FLINT. The Philosophy of History in Europe. By ROBERT FLINT, D.D., LL.D., Professor of Divinity, University of Edinburgh. Vol. I. 8vo. [New Edition in preparation.

—— Theism. Being the Baird Lecture for 1876. By ROBERT FLINT, D.D., LL.D., Professor of Divinity, University of Edinburgh. Seventh Edition. Crown 8vo, 7s. 6d.

—— Anti-Theistic Theories. Being the Baird Lecture for 1877. Fourth Edition. Crown 8vo, 10s. 6d.

—— Agnosticism. Being the Croall Lectures for 1887-88. [In the press.

FORBES. Insulinde: Experiences of a Naturalist's Wife in the Eastern Archipelago. By Mrs H. O. FORBES. Post 8vo, with a Map. 8s. 6d.

FOREIGN CLASSICS FOR ENGLISH READERS. Edited by Mrs OLIPHANT. Price 2s. 6d. *For List of Volumes published, see page 2.*

FOTHERGILL. Diana Wentworth. By CAROLINE FOTHERGILL,
Author of 'An Enthusiast,' &c. 3 vols. post 8vo, 25s. 6d.

FULLARTON. Merlin : A Dramatic Poem. By RALPH MACLEOD
FULLARTON. Crown 8vo, 5s.

GALT. Annals of the Parish. By JOHN GALT. Fcap. 8vo, 2s.
—— The Provost. Fcap. 8vo, 2s.
—— Sir Andrew Wylie. Fcap. 8vo, 2s.
—— The Entail ; or, The Laird of Grippy. Fcap. 8vo, 2s.

GENERAL ASSEMBLY OF THE CHURCH OF SCOTLAND.
—— Family Prayers. Authorised by the General Assembly of
the Church of Scotland. A New Edition, crown 8vo, in large type, 4s. 6d.
Another Edition, crown 8vo, 2s.
—— Prayers for Social and Family Worship. For the Use of
Soldiers, Sailors, Colonists, and Sojourners in India, and other Persons, at
home and abroad, who are deprived of the ordinary services of a Christian
Ministry. New Edition.
—— The Scottish Hymnal Appendix. 1. Longprimer type, 1s.
2. Nonpareil type, cloth limp, 4d.; paper cover, 2d.
—— Scottish Hymnal with Appendix Incorporated. Pub-
lished for Use in Churches by Authority of the General Assembly. 1. Large
type, cloth, red edges, 2s. 6d. ; French morocco, 4s. 2. Bourgeois type, limp
cloth, 1s.; French morocco, 2s. 3. Nonpareil type, cloth, red edges, 6d.;
French morocco, 1s. 4d. 4. Paper covers, 3d. 5. Sunday-School Edition,
paper covers, 1d. 6. Children's Hymnal, paper covers, 1d. No. 1, bound
with the Psalms and Paraphrases, French morocco, 8s. No. 2, bound
with the Psalms and Paraphrases, cloth, 2s. ; French morocco, 3s.

GERARD. Reata : What's in a Name. By E. D. GERARD.
New Edition. Crown 8vo, 6s.
—— Beggar my Neighbour. New Edition. Crown 8vo, 6s.
—— The Waters of Hercules. New Edition. Crown 8vo, 6s.
—— The Land beyond the Forest. Facts, Figures, and
Fancies from Transylvania. By E. GERARD. In Two Volumes. With Maps
and Illustrations. 25s.

GERARD. Stonyhurst Latin Grammar. By Rev. JOHN GERARD.
Fcap. 8vo, 3s.

GILL. Free Trade : an Inquiry into the Nature of its Operation.
By RICHARD GILL. Crown 8vo, 7s. 6d.
—— Free Trade under Protection. Crown 8vo, 7s. 6d.

GOETHE'S FAUST. Translated into English Verse by Sir THEO-
DORE MARTIN, K.C.B. Part I. Second Edition, post 8vo, 6s. Ninth Edition, fcap., 3s. 6d. Part II. Second Edition, revised. Fcap. 8vo, 6s.

GOETHE. Poems and Ballads of Goethe. Translated by Professor
AYTOUN and Sir THEODORE MARTIN, K.C.B. Third Edition, fcap. 8vo, 6s.

GOODALL. Juxta Crucem. Studies of the Love that is over us.
By the late Rev. CHARLES GOODALL, B.D., Minister of Barr. With a Memoir
by Rev. Dr Strong, Glasgow, and Portrait. Crown 8vo, 6s.

GORDON CUMMING. At Home in Fiji. By C. F. GORDON
CUMMING, Author of 'From the Hebrides to the Himalayas.' Fourth Edition,
post 8vo. With Illustrations and Map. 7s. 6d.
—— A Lady's Cruise in a French Man-of-War. New and
Cheaper Edition. 8vo. With Illustrations and Map. 12s. 6d.
—— Fire-Fountains. The Kingdom of Hawaii: Its Volcanoes,
and the History of its Missions. With Map and numerous Illustrations.
2 vols, 8vo, 25s.
—— Wanderings in China. New and Cheaper Edition. 8vo,
with Illustrations, 10s.
—— Granite Crags : The Yŏ-semité Region of California. Illustrated with 8 Engravings. New and Cheaper Edition. 8vo, 8s. 6d.

GRAHAM. The Life and Work of Syed Ahmed Khan, C.S.I.
By Lieut.-Colonel G. F. I. GRAHAM, B.S.C. 8vo, 14s.

GRANT. Bush-Life in Queensland. By A. C. GRANT. New
Edition. Crown 8vo, 6s.

GRIFFITHS. Locked Up. By Major ARTHUR GRIFFITHS.
Author of 'The Wrong Road,' 'Chronicles of Newgate,' &c. With Illustrations
by C. J. STANILAND, R.I. Crown 8vo, 2s. 6d.

HAGGARD. Dodo and I. A Novel. By Captain ANDREW HAGGARD,
D.S.O. Crown 8vo, 6s.

HALDANE. Subtropical Cultivations and Climates. A Handy
Book for Planters, Colonists, and Settlers. By R. C. HALDANE. Post 8vo, 9s.

HALLETT. A Thousand Miles on an Elephant in the Shan States.
By HOLT S. HALLETT, M. Inst. C.E., F.R.G.S., M.R.A.S., Hon. Member Man-
chester and Tyneside Geographical Societies. 8vo, with Maps and numerous
Illustrations, 21s.

HAMERTON. Wenderholme : A Story of Lancashire and Yorkshire Life. By PHILIP GILBERT HAMERTON, Author of 'A Painter's Camp.' A
New Edition. Crown 8vo, 6s.

HAMILTON. Lectures on Metaphysics. By Sir WILLIAM HAMIL-
TON, Bart., Professor of Logic and Metaphysics in the University of Edinburgh.
Edited by the Rev. H. L. MANSEL, B.D., LL.D., Dean of St Paul's ; and JOHN
VEITCH, M.A., Professor of Logic and Rhetoric, Glasgow. Seventh Edition.
2 vols. 8vo, 24s.

—— Lectures on Logic. Edited by the SAME. Third Edition.
2 vols., 24s.

—— Discussions on Philosophy and Literature, Education and
University Reform. Third Edition, 8vo, 21s.

—— Memoir of Sir William Hamilton, Bart., Professor of Logic
and Metaphysics in the University of Edinburgh. By Professor VEITCH, of the
University of Glasgow. 8vo, with Portrait, 18s.

—— Sir William Hamilton: The Man and his Philosophy.
Two Lectures Delivered before the Edinburgh Philosophical Institution,
January and February 1883. By the SAME. Crown 8vo, 2s.

HAMLEY. The Operations of War Explained and Illustrated. By
Lieut.-General Sir EDWARD BRUCE HAMLEY, K.C.B., K.C.M.G., M.P. Fifth
Edition, revised throughout. 4to, with numerous Illustrations, 30s.

—— National Defence ; Articles and Speeches. Post 8vo, 6s.

—— Shakespeare's Funeral, and other Papers. Post 8vo, 7s. 6d.

—— Thomas Carlyle : An Essay. Second Edition. Crown
8vo. 2s. 6d.

—— The Story of the Campaign of Sebastopol. Written in the
Camp. With Illustrations drawn in Camp by the Author. 8vo, 21s.

—— On Outposts. Second Edition. 8vo, 2s.

—— Wellington's Career ; A Military and Political Summary.
Crown 8vo, 2s.

—— Lady Lee's Widowhood. Crown 8vo, 2s. 6d.

—— Our Poor Relations. A Philozoic Essay. With Illustrations, chiefly by Ernest Griset. Crown 8vo, cloth gilt, 3s. 6d.

HAMLEY. Guilty, or Not Guilty? A Tale. By Major-General
W. G. HAMLEY, late of the Royal Engineers. New Edition. Crown 8vo, 3s. 6d.

—— Traseaden Hall. "When George the Third was King."
New and Cheaper Edition. Crown 8vo, 6s.

HARRISON. The Scot in Ulster. The Story of the Scottish
Settlement in Ulster. By JOHN HARRISON, Author of 'Oure Tounis Col-
ledge.' Crown 8vo, 2s. 6d.

HASELL. Bible Partings. By E. J. HASELL. Crown 8vo, 6s.

—— Short Family Prayers. Cloth, 1s.

HAY. The Works of the Right Rev. Dr George Hay, Bishop of
Edinburgh. Edited under the Supervision of the Right Rev. Bishop STRAIN.
With Memoir and Portrait of the Author. 5 vols. crown 8vo, bound in extra
cloth, £1, 1s. Or, sold separately—viz. :
The Sincere Christian Instructed in the Faith of Christ from the Written Word.
2 vols., 8s.—The Devout Christian Instructed in the Law of Christ from the Written
Word. 2 vols., 8s.—The Pious Christian Instructed in the Nature and Practice of the
Principal Exercises of Piety. 1 vol., 4s.

HEATLEY. The Horse-Owner's Safeguard. A Handy Medical
Guide for every Man who owns a Horse. By G. S. HEATLEY, M.R.C.V.S.
Crown 8vo, 5s.

—— The Stock-Owner's Guide. A Handy Medical Treatise for
every Man who owns an Ox or a Cow. Crown 8vo, 4s. 6d.   ʼ

HEDDERWICK. Lays of Middle Age; and other Poems. By
JAMES HEDDERWICK, LL.D. Price 3s. 6d.

HEMANS.—The Poetical Works of Mrs Hemans. Copyright Edi-
tions.—One Volume, royal 8vo, 5s.—The Same, with Illustrations engraved on
Steel, bound in cloth, gilt edges, 7s. 6d.—Six Volumes in Three, fcap., 12s. 6d.
SELECT POEMS OF MRS HEMANS. Fcap., cloth, gilt edges, 3s.

HOME PRAYERS. By Ministers of the Church of Scotland and
Members of the Church Service Society. Second Edition. Fcap. 8vo, 3s.

HOMER. The Odyssey. Translated into English Verse in the
Spenserian Stanza. By PHILIP STANHOPE WORSLEY. Third Edition, 2 vols.
fcap., 12s.

—— The Iliad. Translated by P. S. WORSLEY and Professor
CONINGTON. 2 vols. crown 8vo, 21s.

HOSACK. Mary Queen of Scots and Her Accusers. Containing a
Variety of Documents never before published. By JOHN HOSACK, Barrister-
at-Law. A New and Enlarged Edition, with a Photograph from the Bust on
the Tomb in Westminster Abbey. 2 vols. 8vo, £1, 11s. 6d.

HUTCHINSON. Hints on the Game of Golf. By HORACE G.
HUTCHINSON. Fourth Edition. Fcap. 8vo, cloth, 1s. 6d.

IDDESLEIGH. Lectures and Essays. By the late EARL OF
IDDESLEIGH, G.C.B., D.C.L., &c. 8vo, 16s.

INDEX GEOGRAPHICUS : Being a List, alphabetically arranged,
of the Principal Places on the Globe, with the Countries and Subdivisions of
the Countries in which they are situated, and their Latitudes and Longitudes.
Applicable to all Modern Atlases and Maps. Imperial 8vo, pp. 676, 21s.

JAMIESON. Discussions on the Atonement: Is it Vicarious ?
By the Rev. GEORGE JAMIESON, A.M., B.D., D.D., Author of 'Profound Problems in Philosophy and Theology,' 8vo, 16s.

JEAN JAMBON. Our Trip to Blunderland ; or, Grand Excursion
to Blundertown and Back. By JEAN JAMBON. With Sixty Illustrations
designed by CHARLES DOYLE, engraved by DALZIEL. Fourth Thousand.
Cloth, gilt edges, 6s. 6d. Cheap Edition, cloth, 3s. 6d. Boards, 2s. 6d.

JENNINGS. Mr Gladstone: A Study. By LOUIS J. JENNINGS,
M.P., Author of 'Republican Government in the United States,' 'The Croker
Memoirs,' &c. Popular Edition. Crown 8vo, 1s.

JERNINGHAM. Reminiscences of an Attaché. By HUBERT
E. H. JERNINGHAM. Second Edition. Crown 8vo, 5s.

—— Diane de Breteuille. A Love Story. Crown 8vo, 2s. 6d.

JOHNSTON. The Chemistry of Common Life. By Professor
J. F. W. JOHNSTON. New Edition, Revised, and brought down to date. By
ARTHUR HERBERT CHURCH, M.A. Oxon.; Author of 'Food: its Sources,
Constituents, and Uses,' &c., &c. Illustrated with Maps and 102 Engravings
on Wood. Complete in one volume, crown 8vo, 7s. 6d.

—— Elements of Agricultural Chemistry and Geology. Revised, and brought down to date. By Sir CHARLES A. CAMERON, M.D.,
F.R.C.S.I., &c. Fifteenth Edition. Fcap. 8vo, 6s. 6d.

JOHNSTON. Catechism of Agricultural Chemistry and Geology.
An entirely New Edition, revised and enlarged, by Sir CHARLES A. CAMERON, M.D., F.R.C.S.I.,&c. Eighty-sixth Thousand, with numerous Illustrations, 1s.

JOHNSTON. Patrick Hamilton : a Tragedy of the Reformation
in Scotland, 1528. By T. P. JOHNSTON. Crown 8vo, with Two Etchings. 5s.

KENNEDY. Sport, Travel, and Adventures in Newfoundland
and the West Indies. By Captain W. R. KENNEDY, R.N. With Illustrations by the Author. Post 8vo. 14s.

KER. Short Studies on St Paul's Letter to the Philippians. By
Rev. WILLIAM LEE KER, Minister of Kilwinning. Crown 8vo, 5s.

KING. The Metamorphoses of Ovid. Translated in English Blank
Verse. By HENRY KING, M.A., Fellow of Wadham College, Oxford, and of the Inner Temple, Barrister-at-Law. Crown 8vo, 10s. 6d.

KINGLAKE. History of the Invasion of the Crimea. By A. W.
KINGLAKE. Cabinet Edition, revised. Illustrated with Maps and Plans. Complete in 9 Vols., crown 8vo, at 6s. each. The Vols. respectively contain : I. THE ORIGIN OF THE WAR. II. RUSSIA MET AND INVADED. III. THE BATTLE OF THE ALMA. IV. SEBASTOPOL AT BAY. V. THE BATTLE OF BALACLAVA. VI. THE BATTLE OF INKERMAN. VII. WINTER TROUBLES. VIII. and IX. FROM THE MORROW OF INKERMAN TO THE DEATH OF LORD RAGLAN. With an Index to the Complete Work.

—— History of the Invasion of the Crimea. Demy 8vo. Vol.
VI. Winter Troubles. With a Map, 16s. Vols. VII. and VIII. From the Morrow of Inkerman to the Death of Lord Raglan. With an Index to the Whole Work. With Maps and Plans. 28s.

—— Eothen. A New Edition, uniform with the Cabinet Edition
of the 'History of the Invasion of the Crimea,' price 6s.

KNOLLYS. The Elements of Field-Artillery. Designed for the
Use of Infantry and Cavalry Officers. By HENRY KNOLLYS, Captain Royal Artillery; Author of 'From Sedan to Saarbrück,' Editor of 'Incidents in the Sepoy War,' &c. With Engravings. Crown 8vo, 7s. 6d.

LAVERGNE. The Rural Economy of England, Scotland, and Ire-
land. By LEONCE DE LAVERGNE. Translated from the French. With Notes by a Scottish Farmer. 8vo, 12s.

LAWLESS. Hurrish : a Study. By the Hon. EMILY LAWLESS,
Author of 'A Chelsea Householder,' &c. Fourth Edition, crown 8vo, 6s.

LEE. A Phantom Lover : a Fantastic Story. By VERNON LEE.
Crown 8vo, 1s.

LEE. Glimpses in the Twilight. Being various Notes, Records,
and Examples of the Supernatural. By the Rev. GEORGE F. LEE, D.C.L. Crown 8vo. 8s. 6d.

LEES. A Handbook of Sheriff Court Styles. By J. M. LEES,
M.A., LL.B., Advocate, Sheriff-Substitute of Lanarkshire. New Ed., 8vo, 21s.

—— A Handbook of the Sheriff and Justice of Peace Small
Debt Courts. 8vo. 7s. 6d.

LETTERS FROM THE HIGHLANDS. Reprinted from 'The
Times.' Fcap. 8vo, 4s. 6d.

LIGHTFOOT. Studies in Philosophy. By the Rev. J. LIGHTFOOT,
M.A., D.Sc., Vicar of Cross Stone, Todmorden. Crown 8vo, 4s. 6d.

LITTLE HAND AND MUCKLE GOLD. A Study of To-day.
In 3 vols. post 8vo, 25s. 6d.

LOCKHART. Doubles and Quits. By LAURENCE W. M. LOCK-
HART. With Twelve Illustrations. Fourth Edition. Crown 8vo, 6s.

—— Fair to See : a Novel. Eighth Edition. Crown 8vo, 6s.

—— Mine is Thine : a Novel. Eighth Edition. Crown 8vo, 6s.

LORIMER. The Institutes of Law : A Treatise of the Principles
of Jurisprudence as determined by Nature. By JAMES LORIMER, Regius Professor of Public Law and of the Law of Nature and Nations in the University of Edinburgh. New Edition, revised and much enlarged. 8vo, 18s.

LORIMER. The Institutes of the Law of Nations. A Treatise of the Jural Relation of Separate Political Communities. In 2 vols. 8vo. Volume I. price 16s. Volume II., price 20s.

LYSTER. Another Such Victory! By ANNETTE LYSTER, Author of 'A Leal Light Heart,' 'Two Old Maids,' &c. 3 vols. crown 8vo, 25s. 6d.

M'COMBIE. Cattle and Cattle-Breeders. By WILLIAM M'COMBIE, Tillyfour. New Edition, enlarged, with Memoir of the Author. By JAMES MACDONALD, of the 'Farming World.' Crown 8vo, 3s. 6d.

MACRAE. A Handbook of Deer-Stalking. By ALEXANDER MACRAE, late Forester to Lord Henry Bentinck. With Introduction by HORATIO ROSS, Esq. Fcap. 8vo, with two Photographs from Life. 3s. 6d.

M'CRIE. Works of the Rev. Thomas M'Crie, D.D. Uniform Edition. Four vols. crown 8vo, 24s.
—— Life of John Knox. Containing Illustrations of the History of the Reformation in Scotland. Crown 8vo, 6s. Another Edition, 3s. 6d.
—— Life of Andrew Melville. Containing Illustrations of the Ecclesiastical and Literary History of Scotland in the Sixteenth and Seventeenth Centuries. Crown 8vo, 6s.
—— History of the Progress and Suppression of the Reformation in Italy in the Sixteenth Century. Crown 8vo, 4s.
—— History of the Progress and Suppression of the Reformation in Spain in the Sixteenth Century. Crown 8vo, 3s. 6d.
—— Lectures on the Book of Esther. Fcap. 8vo, 5s.

MACDONALD. A Manual of the Criminal Law (Scotland) Procedure Act, 1887. By NORMAN DORAN MACDONALD. Revised by the LORD JUSTICE-CLERK. 8vo, cloth, 10s. 6d.

MACGREGOR. Life and Opinions of Major-General Sir Charles MacGregor, K.C.B., C.S.I., C.I.E, Quartermaster-General of India. From his Letters and Diaries. Edited by LADY MACGREGOR. With Portraits and Maps to illustrate Campaigns in which he was engaged. 2 vols. 8vo, 35s.

M'INTOSH. The Book of the Garden. By CHARLES M'INTOSH, formerly Curator of the Royal Gardens of his Majesty the King of the Belgians, and lately of those of his Grace the Duke of Buccleuch, K.G., at Dalkeith Palace. 2 vols. royal 8vo, with 1350 Engravings. £4, 7s. 6d. Vol. I. On the Formation of Gardens and Construction of Garden Edifices. £2, 10s. Vol. II. Practical Gardening. £1, 17s. 6d.

MACINTYRE. Hindu Koh: Wanderings and Wild Sports on and beyond the Himalayas. By Major-General DONALD MACINTYRE, V.C., late Prince of Wales' Own Goorkhas, F.R.G.S. Dedicated to H.R.H. The Prince of Wales. 8vo, with numerous Illustrations, 21s.

MACKAY. A Manual of Modern Geography; Mathematical, Physical, and Political. By the Rev. ALEXANDER MACKAY, LL.D., F.R.G.S. 11th Thousand, revised to the present time. Crown 8vo, pp. 688. 7s. 6d.
—— Elements of Modern Geography. 53d Thousand, revised to the present time. Crown 8vo, pp. 300, 3s.
—— The Intermediate Geography. By the Rev. ALEXANDER MACKAY, LL.D., F.R.G.S. Intended as an Intermediate Book between the Author's 'Outlines of Geography' and 'Elements of Geography,' Fifteenth Edition, revised. Crown 8vo, pp. 238, 2s.
—— Outlines of Modern Geography. 186th Thousand, revised to the present time. 18mo, pp. 118, 1s.
—— First Steps in Geography. 105th Thousand. 18mo, pp. 56. Sewed, 4d.; cloth, 6d.
—— Elements of Physiography and Physical Geography. With Express Reference to the Instructions recently issued by the Science and Art Department. 30th Thousand, revised. Crown 8vo, 1s. 6d.
—— Facts and Dates; or, the Leading Events in Sacred and Profane History, and the Principal Facts in the various Physical Sciences. The Memory being aided throughout by a Simple and Natural Method. For Schools and Private Reference. New Edition. Crown 8vo, 3s. 6d.

MACKAY. An Old Scots Brigade. Being the History of Mackay's Regiment, now incorporated with the Royal Scots. With an Appendix containing many Original Documents connected with the History of the Regiment. By JOHN MACKAY (late) OF HERRIESDALE. Crown 8vo, 5s.

MACKAY. The Founders of the American Republic. A History of Washington, Adams, Jefferson, Franklin, and Madison. With a Supplementary Chapter on the Inherent Causes of the Ultimate Failure of American Democracy. By CHARLES MACKAY, LL.D. Post 8vo, 10s. 6d.

MACKENZIE. Studies in Roman Law. With Comparative Views of the Laws of France, England, and Scotland. By LORD MACKENZIE, one of the Judges of the Court of Session in Scotland. Sixth Edition, Edited by JOHN KIRKPATRICK, Esq., M.A. Cantab.; Dr Jur. Heidelb.; LL.B. Edin.; Advocate. 8vo, 12s.

MAIN. Three Hundred English Sonnets. Chosen and Edited by DAVID M. MAIN. Fcap. 8vo, 6s.

MAIR. A Digest of Laws and Decisions, Ecclesiastical and Civil, relating to the Constitution, Practice, and Affairs of the Church of Scotland. With Notes and Forms of Procedure. By the Rev. WILLIAM MAIR, D.D., Minister of the Parish of Earlston. Crown 8vo. With Supplements, 8s.

MARMORNE. The Story is told by ADOLPHUS SEGRAVE, the youngest of three Brothers. Third Edition. Crown 8vo, 6s.

MARSHALL. French Home Life. By FREDERIC MARSHALL. Second Edition. 5s.

MARSHMAN. History of India. From the Earliest Period to the Close of the India Company's Government; with an Epitome of Subsequent Events. By JOHN CLARK MARSHMAN, C.S.I. Abridged from the Author's larger work. Second Edition, revised. Crown 8vo, with Map, 6s. 6d.

MARTIN. Goethe's Faust. Part I. Translated by Sir THEODORE MARTIN, K.C.B. Second Ed., crown 8vo, 6s. Ninth Ed., fcap. 8vo, 3s. 6d.

———— Goethe's Faust. Part II. Translated into English Verse. Second Edition, revised. Fcap. 8vo, 6s.

———— The Works of Horace. Translated into English Verse, with Life and Notes. 2 vols. New Edition, crown 8vo, 21s.

———— Poems and Ballads of Heinrich Heine. Done into English Verse. Second Edition. Printed on *papier vergé*, crown 8vo, 8s.

———— The Song of the Bell, and other Translations from Schiller, Goethe, Uhland, and Others. Crown 8vo, 7s. 6d.

———— Catullus. With Life and Notes. Second Ed., post 8vo, 7s. 6d.

———— Aladdin : A Dramatic Poem. By ADAM OEHLENSCHLAEGER. Fcap. 8vo, 5s.

———— Correggio : A Tragedy. By OEHLENSCHLAEGER. With Notes. Fcap. 8vo, 3s.

———— King Rene's Daughter : A Danish Lyrical Drama. By HENRIK HERTZ. Second Edition, fcap., 2s. 6d.

MARTIN. On some of Shakespeare's Female Characters. In a Series of Letters. By HELENA FAUCIT, LADY MARTIN. Dedicated by permission to Her Most Gracious Majesty the Queen. Third Edition. 8vo, with Portrait, 7s. 6d.

MATHESON. Can the Old Faith Live with the New? or the Problem of Evolution and Revelation. By the Rev. GEORGE MATHESON, D.D. Third Edition. Crown 8vo, 7s. 6d.

———— The Psalmist and the Scientist; or, Modern Value of the Religious Sentiment. Crown 8vo, 7s. 6d.

———— Sacred Songs. Crown 8vo, 5s.

MAURICE. The Balance of Military Power in Europe. An Examination of the War Resources of Great Britain and the Continental States. By Colonel MAURICE, R.A., Professor of Military Art and History at the Royal Staff College. Crown 8vo, with a Map. 6s.

MICHEL. A Critical Inquiry into the Scottish Language. With the view of Illustrating the Rise and Progress of Civilisation in Scotland. By FRANCISQUE-MICHEL, F.S.A. Lond. and Scot., Correspondant de l'Institut de France, &c. 4to, printed on hand-made paper, and bound in Roxburghe, 66s.

MICHIE. The Larch : Being a Practical Treatise on its Culture and General Management. By CHRISTOPHER Y. MICHIE, Forester, Cullen House. Crown 8vo, with Illustrations. New and Cheaper Edition, enlarged, 5s.

—— Practical Forestry. Crown 8vo, with Illustrations. 6s.

MIDDLETON. The Story of Alastair Bhan Comyn ; or, The Tragedy of Dunphail. A Tale of Tradition and Romance. By the Lady MIDDLETON. Square 8vo, 10s.

MILNE. The Problem of the Churchless and Poor in our Large Towns. With special reference to the Home Mission Work of the Church of Scotland. By the Rev. ROBT. MILNE, M.A., D.D., Ardler. Crown 8vo, 3s. 6d.

MINTO. A Manual of English Prose Literature, Biographical and Critical : designed mainly to show Characteristics of Style. By W. MINTO, M.A., Professor of Logic in the University of Aberdeen. Third Edition, revised. Crown 8vo, 7s. 6d.

—— Characteristics of English Poets, from Chaucer to Shirley. New Edition, revised. Crown 8vo, 7s. 6d.

MITCHELL. Biographies of Eminent Soldiers of the last Four Centuries. By Major-General JOHN MITCHELL, Author of 'Life of Wallenstein.' With a Memoir of the Author. 8vo, 9s

MOIR. Life of Mansie Wauch, Tailor in Dalkeith. With 8 Illustrations on Steel, by the late GEORGE CRUIKSHANK. Crown 8vo, 3s. 6d. Another Edition, fcap. 8vo, 1s. 6d.

MOMERIE. Defects of Modern Christianity, and other Sermons. By ALFRED WILLIAMS MOMERIE, M.A., D.Sc., LL.D., Professor of Logic and Metaphysics in King's College, London. Third Edition. Crown 8vo, 5s.

—— The Basis of Religion. Being an Examination of Natural Religion. Second Edition. Crown 8vo, 2s. 6d.

—— The Origin of Evil, and other Sermons. Sixth Edition, enlarged. Crown 8vo, 5s.

—— Personality. The Beginning and End of Metaphysics, and a Necessary Assumption in all Positive Philosophy. Fourth Ed. Cr. 8vo, 3s.

—— Agnosticism. Second Edition, Revised. Crown 8vo. 5s.

—— Preaching and Hearing ; and other Sermons. Second Edition. Crown 8vo, 4s. 6d.

—— Belief in God. Second Edition. Crown 8vo, 3s.

—— Inspiration ; and other Sermons. Crown 8vo, 5s.

—— Church and Creed. Crown 8vo, 4s. 6d.

MONTAGUE. Campaigning in South Africa. Reminiscences of an Officer in 1879. By Captain W. E. MONTAGUE, 94th Regiment, Author of 'Claude Meadowleigh,' &c. 8vo, 10s. 6d.

MONTALEMBERT. Memoir of Count de Montalembert. A Chapter of Recent French History. By Mrs OLIPHANT, Author of the 'Life of Edward Irving.' &c. 2 vols. crown 8vo. £1. 4s

MORISON. Sordello. An Outline Analysis of Mr Browning's Poem. By JEANIE MORISON, Author of 'The Purposes of the Ages,' 'Ane Book of Ballades,' &c. Crown 8vo, 3s.

MURDOCH. Manual of the Law of Insolvency and Bankruptcy : Comprehending a Summary of the Law of Insolvency, Notour Bankruptcy, Composition-contracts, Trust-deeds, Cessio, and Sequestrations ; and the Winding-up of Joint-Stock Companies in Scotland ; with Annotations on the various Insolvency and Bankruptcy Statutes ; and with Forms of Procedure applicable to these Subjects. By JAMES MURDOCH, Member of the Faculty of Procurators in Glasgow. Fifth Edition, Revised and Enlarged, 8vo, £1, 10s.

MY TRIVIAL LIFE AND MISFORTUNE: A Gossip with
no Plot in Particular. By A PLAIN WOMAN. New Edition, crown 8vo, 6s.
By the SAME AUTHOR.
POOR NELLIE. New and Cheaper Edition. Crown 8vo, 6s.

NAPIER. The Construction of the Wonderful Canon of Logar-
ithms (Mirifici Logarithmorum Canonis Constructio). By JOHN NAPIER of
Merchiston. Translated for the first time, with Notes, and a Catalogue of
Napier's Works, by WILLIAM RAE MACDONALD. Small 4to, 15s. *A few large
paper copies may be had, printed on Whatman paper, price 30s.*

NEAVES. Songs and Verses, Social and Scientific. By an Old
Contributor to 'Maga.' By the Hon. Lord NEAVES. Fifth Ed., fcap. 8vo, 4s.
——— The Greek Anthology. Being Vol. XX. of 'Ancient Clas-
sics for English Readers.' Crown 8vo, 2s. 6d.

NICHOLSON. A Manual of Zoology, for the Use of Students.
With a General Introduction on the Principles of Zoology. By HENRY AL-
LEYNE NICHOLSON, M.D., D.Sc., F.L.S., F.G.S., Regius Professor of Natural
History in the University of Aberdeen. Seventh Edition, rewritten and
enlarged. Post 8vo, pp. 956, with 555 Engravings on Wood, 18s.
——— Text-Book of Zoology, for the Use of Schools. Fourth Edi-
tion, enlarged. Crown 8vo, with 188 Engravings on Wood, 7s. 6d.
——— Introductory Text-Book of Zoology, for the Use of Junior
Classes. Sixth Edition, revised and enlarged, with 166 Engravings, 3s.
——— Outlines of Natural History, for Beginners ; being Descrip-
tions of a Progressive Series of Zoological Types. Third Edition, with
Engravings, 1s. 6d.
——— A Manual of Palæontology, for the Use of Students.
With a General Introduction on the Principles of Palæontology. By Professor
H. ALLEYNE NICHOLSON and RICHARD LYDEKKER. Third Edition. Rewritten
and greatly enlarged. 2 vols. 8vo, with Engravings, £3 3s.
——— The Ancient Life-History of the Earth. An Outline of
the Principles and Leading Facts of Palæontological Science. Crown 8vo,
with 276 Engravings, 10s. 6d.
——— On the "Tabulate Corals" of the Palæozoic Period, with
Critical Descriptions of Illustrative Species. Illustrated with 15 Litho-
graph Plates and numerous Engravings. Super-royal 8vo, 21s.
——— Synopsis of the Classification of the Animal King-
dom. 8vo, with 106 Illustrations, 6s.
——— On the Structure and Affinities of the Genus Monticuli-
pora and its Sub-Genera, with Critical Descriptions of Illustrative Species.
Illustrated with numerous Engravings on wood and lithographed Plates.
Super-royal 8vo, 18s.

NICHOLSON. Communion with Heaven, and other Sermons.
By the late MAXWELL NICHOLSON, D.D., Minister of St Stephen's, Edinburgh
Crown 8vo, 5s. 6d.
——— Rest in Jesus. Sixth Edition. Fcap. 8vo, 4s. 6d.

NICHOLSON. A Treatise on Money, and Essays on Present
Monetary Problems. By JOSEPH SHIELD NICHOLSON, M.A., D.Sc., Professor
of Commercial and Political Economy and Mercantile Law in the University
of Edinburgh. 8vo, 10s. 6d.

NICOLSON AND MURE. A Handbook to the Local Govern-
ment (Scotland) Act, 1889. With Introduction, Explanatory Notes, and
Index. By J. BADENACH NICOLSON, Advocate, Counsel to the Scotch Education Department, and W. J. MURE, Advocate, Legal Secretary to the Lord
Advocate for Scotland. Seventh Reprint. 8vo, 5s.

OLIPHANT. Masollam: a Problem of the Period. A Novel.
By LAURENCE OLIPHANT. 3 vols. post 8vo, 25s. 6d.
——— Scientific Religion ; or, Higher Possibilities of Life and
Practice through the Operation of Natural Forces. Second Edition. 8vo, 16s.

OLIPHANT. Altiora Peto. New and Cheaper Edition. Crown
8vo, boards, 2s. 6d. Illustrated Edition. Crown 8vo, cloth, 6s.
——— Piccadilly : A Fragment of Contemporary Biography. With
Eight Illustrations by Richard Doyle. Eighth Edition, 4s. 6d. Cheap Edition,
in paper cover, 2s. 6d.
——— Traits and Travesties ; Social and Political. Post 8vo, 10s. 6d.
——— The Land of Gilead. With Excursions in the Lebanon.
With Illustrations and Maps. Demy 8vo, 21s.
——— The Land of Khemi. Post 8vo, with Illustrations, 10s. 6d.
——— Haifa : Life in Modern Palestine. 2d Edition. 8vo, 7s. 6d.
——— Episodes in a Life of Adventure ; or, Moss from a Rolling
Stone. Fourth Edition. Post 8vo, 6s.
——— Fashionable Philosophy, and other Sketches. In paper
cover, 1s.
——— Sympneumata : or, Evolutionary Functions now Active in
Man. Edited by LAURENCE OLIPHANT. Post 8vo, 10s. 6d.
OLIPHANT. Katie Stewart. By Mrs Oliphant. 2s. 6d.
OSBORN. Narratives of Voyage and Adventure. By Admiral
SHERARD OSBORN, C.B. 3 vols. crown 8vo, 12s.
OSSIAN. The Poems of Ossian in the Original Gaelic. With a
Literal Translation into English, and a Dissertation on the Authenticity of the
Poems. By the Rev. ARCHIBALD CLERK. 2 vols. imperial 8vo, £1, 11s. 6d.
OSWALD. By Fell and Fjord ; or, Scenes and Studies in Iceland.
By E. J. OSWALD. Post 8vo, with Illustrations. 7s. 6d.
OUTRAM. Lyrics : Legal and Miscellaneous. By the late GEORGE
OUTRAM, Esq., Advocate. New Edition, with Explanatory Notes. Edited
by J. H. Stoddart, LL.D. and Illustrated by William Ralston and A. S.
Boyd. Fcap. 8vo, 5s.
PAGE. Introductory Text-Book of Geology. By DAVID PAGE,
LL.D., Professor of Geology in the Durham University of Physical Science,
Newcastle, and Professor LAPWORTH of Mason Science College, Birmingham.
With Engravings and Glossarial Index. Twelfth Edition. Revised and En-
larged. 3s. 6d.
——— Advanced Text-Book of Geology, Descriptive and Indus-
trial. With Engravings, and Glossary of Scientific Terms. Sixth Edition, re-
vised and enlarged, 7s. 6d.
——— Introductory Text-Book of Physical Geography. With
Sketch-Maps and Illustrations. Edited by CHARLES LAPWORTH, LL.D., F.G.S.,
&c., Professor of Geology and Mineralogy in the Mason Science College, Bir-
mingham. 12th Edition. 2s. 6d.
——— Advanced Text-Book of Physical Geography. Third
Edition, Revised and Enlarged by Prof. LAPWORTH. With Engravings. 5s.
PATON. Spindrift. By Sir J. NOEL PATON. Fcap., cloth, 5s.
——— Poems by a Painter. Fcap., cloth, 5s.
PATON. Body and Soul. A Romance in Transcendental Path-
ology. By FREDERICK NOEL PATON. Third Edition. Crown 8vo, 1s.
PATTERSON. Essays in History and Art. By R. HOGARTH
PATTERSON. 8vo, 12s.
——— The New Golden Age, and Influence of the Precious
Metals upon the World. 2 vols. 8vo, 31s. 6d.
PAUL. History of the Royal Company of Archers, the Queen's
Body-Guard for Scotland. By JAMES BALFOUR PAUL, Advocate of the Scottish
Bar. Crown 4to, with Portraits and other Illustrations. £2, 2s.
PEILE. Lawn Tennis as a Game of Skill. With latest revised
Laws as played by the Best Clubs. By Captain S. C. F. PEILE, B.S.C. Fourth
Edition, fcap. cloth, 1s. 6d
PETTIGREW. The Handy Book of Bees, and their Profitable
Management. By A. PETTIGREW. Fifth Edition, Enlarged, with Engrav-
ings. Crown 8vo, 3s. 6d.

PHILOSOPHICAL CLASSICS FOR ENGLISH READERS. Companion Series to Ancient and Foreign Classics for English Readers. Edited by WILLIAM KNIGHT, LL.D., Professor of Moral Philosophy, University of St Andrews. In crown 8vo volumes, with portraits, price 3s. 6d.
[For list of Volumes published, see page 2.

POLLOK. The Course of Time : A Poem. By ROBERT POLLOK, A.M. Small fcap. 8vo, cloth gilt, 2s. 6d. The Cottage Edition, 32mo, sewed, 8d. The Same, cloth, gilt edges, 1s. 6d. Another Edition, with Illustrations by Birket Foster and others, fcap., gilt cloth, 3s. 6d., or with edges gilt, 4s.

PORT ROYAL LOGIC. Translated from the French ; with Introduction, Notes, and Appendix. By THOMAS SPENCER BAYNES, LL.D., Professor in the University of St Andrews. Tenth Edition, 12mo, 4s.

POTTS AND DARNELL. Aditus Faciliores : An easy Latin Construing Book, with Complete Vocabulary. By A. W. POTTS, M.A., LL.D., Head-Master of the Fettes College, Edinburgh ; and the Rev. C. DARNELL, M.A., Head-Master of Cargilfield Preparatory School, Edinburgh. Tenth Edition, fcap. 8vo, 3s. 6d.

——— Aditus Faciliores Graeci. An easy Greek Construing Book, with Complete Vocabulary. Fourth Edition, fcap. 8vo, 3s.

PRINGLE. The Live-Stock of the Farm. By ROBERT O. PRINGLE. Third Edition. Revised and Edited by JAMES MACDONALD, of the 'Farming World,' &c. Crown 8vo, 7s. 6d.

PUBLIC GENERAL STATUTES AFFECTING SCOTLAND from 1707 to 1847, with Chronological Table and Index. 3 vols. large 8vo, £3, 3s.

PUBLIC GENERAL STATUTES AFFECTING SCOTLAND, COLLECTION OF. Published Annually with General Index.

RAMSAY. Rough Recollections of Military Service and Society. By Lieut.-Col. BALCARRES D. WARDLAW RAMSAY. Two vols. post 8vo, 21s.

RAMSAY. Scotland and Scotsmen in the Eighteenth Century. Edited from the MSS. of JOHN RAMSAY, Esq. of Ochtertyre, by ALEXANDER ALLARDYCE, Author of 'Memoir of Admiral Lord Keith, K.B.,' &c. 2 vols. 8vo, 31s. 6d.

RANKIN. A Handbook of the Church of Scotland. By JAMES RANKIN, D.D., Minister of Muthill; Author of 'Character Studies in the Old Testament,' &c. An entirely New and much Enlarged Edition. Crown 8vo, with 2 Maps, 7s. 6d.

RANKINE. A Treatise on the Rights and Burdens incident to the Ownership of Lands and other Heritages in Scotland. By JOHN RANKINE, M.A., Advocate, Professor of Scots Law in the University of Edinburgh. Second Edition, Revised and Enlarged. 8vo, 45s.

RECORDS OF THE TERCENTENARY FESTIVAL OF THE UNIVERSITY OF EDINBURGH. Celebrated in April 1884. Published under the Sanction of the Senatus Academicus. Large 4to, £2, 12s. 6d.

RICE. Reminiscences of Abraham Lincoln. By Distinguished Men of his Time. Collected and Edited by ALLEN THORNDIKE RICE, Editor of the 'North American Review.' Large 8vo, with Portraits, 21s.

ROBERTSON. Orellana, and other Poems. By J. LOGIE ROBERTSON, M.A. Fcap. 8vo. Printed on hand-made paper. 6s.

ROBERTSON. Our Holiday Among the Hills. By JAMES and JANET LOGIE ROBERTSON. Fcap. 8vo, 3s. 6d.

ROSCOE. Rambles with a Fishing-rod. By E. S. ROSCOE. Crown 8vo, 4s. 6d.

ROSS. Old Scottish Regimental Colours. By ANDREW ROSS, S.S.C., Hon. Secretary Old Scottish Regimental Colours Committee. Dedicated by Special Permission to Her Majesty the Queen. Folio. £2, 12s. 6d.

RUSSELL. The Haigs of Bemersyde. A Family History. By JOHN RUSSELL. Large 8vo, with Illustrations. 21s.

RUSSELL. Fragments from Many Tables. Being the Recollections of some Wise and Witty Men and Women. By GEO. RUSSELL. Cr. 8vo, 4s. 6d.

RUSSELL. Essays on Sacred Subjects for General Readers. By the Rev. WILLIAM RUSSELL, M.A. 8vo, 10s. 6d.

RUSTOW. The War for the Rhine Frontier, 1870. By Col. W. RUSTOW. Translated from the German, by JOHN LAYLAND NEEDHAM, Lieutenant R.M. Artillery. 3 vols. 8vo, with Maps and Plans, £1, 11s. 6d.

RUTLAND. Notes of an Irish Tour in 1846. By the DUKE OF RUTLAND, G.C.B. (Lord JOHN MANNERS). New Edition. Crown 8vo, 2s. 6d.

RUTLAND. Gems of German Poetry. Translated by the DUCHESS OF RUTLAND (Lady JOHN MANNERS). New Edition in preparation.

------ Impressions of Bad-Homburg. Comprising a Short Account of the Women's Associations of Germany under the Red Cross. Crown 8vo, 1s. 6d.

------ Some Personal Recollections of the Later Years of the Earl of Beaconsfield, K.G. Sixth Edition, 6d.

------ Employment of Women in the Public Service. 6d.

------ Some of the Advantages of Easily Accessible Reading and Recreation Rooms, and Free Libraries. With Remarks on Starting and Maintaining Them. Second Edition, crown 8vo, 1s.

------ A Sequel to Rich Men's Dwellings, and other Occasional Papers. Crown 8vo, 2s. 6d.

------ Encouraging Experiences of Reading and Recreation Rooms, Aims of Guilds, Nottingham Social Guild, Existing Institutions, &c., &c. Crown 8vo, 1s.

SCHILLER. Wallenstein. A Dramatic Poem. By FREDERICK VON SCHILLER. Translated by C. G. A. LOCKHART. Fcap. 8vo, 7s. 6d.

SCOTCH LOCH FISHING. By "Black Palmer." Crown 8vo, interleaved with blank pages, 4s.

SCOUGAL. Scenes from a Silent World; or, Prisons and their Inmates. By FRANCIS SCOUGAL. Crown 8vo, 6s.

SELLAR. Manual of the Education Acts for Scotland. By ALEXANDER CRAIG SELLAR, M.P. Eighth Edition. Revised and in great part rewritten by J. EDWARD GRAHAM, B.A. Oxon., Advocate. Containing the Technical Schools Act, 1887, and all Acts bearing on Education in Scotland. With Rules for the conduct of Elections, with Notes and Cases. With a Supplement, being the Acts of 1889 in so far as affecting the Education Acts. 8vo, 12s. 6d.

[SUPPLEMENT TO SELLAR'S MANUAL OF THE EDUCATION ACTS FOR SCOTLAND. 8vo, 2s.]

SELLER AND STEPHENS. Physiology at the Farm; in Aid of Rearing and Feeding the Live Stock. By WILLIAM SELLER, M.D., F.R.S.E., and HENRY STEPHENS, F.R.S.E., Author of 'The Book of the Farm,' &c. Post 8vo, with Engravings, 16s.

SETH. Scottish Philosophy. A Comparison of the Scottish and German Answers to Hume. Balfour Philosophical Lectures, University of Edinburgh. By ANDREW SETH, M.A., Professor of Logic, Rhetoric, and Metaphysics in the University of St Andrews. Second Edition. Crown 8vo, 5s.

------ Hegelianism and Personality. Balfour Philosophical Lectures. Second Series. Crown 8vo, 5s.

SETON. A Budget of Anecdotes. Chiefly relating to the Current Century. Compiled and Arranged by GEORGE SETON, Advocate, M.A. Oxon. New and Cheaper Edition, fcap. 8vo. Boards, 1s. 6d.

SHADWELL. The Life of Colin Campbell, Lord Clyde. Illustrated by Extracts from his Diary and Correspondence. By Lieutenant-General SHADWELL, C.B. 2 vols. 8vo. With Portrait, Maps, and Plans. 36s.

SHAND. Half a Century; or, Changes in Men and Manners. By ALEX. INNES SHAND, Author of 'Against Time,' &c. Second Ed., 8vo, 12s. 6d.

------ Letters from the West of Ireland. Reprinted from the 'Times.' Crown 8vo, 5s.

SHARPE. Letters from and to Charles Kirkpatrick Sharpe.
Edited by ALEXANDER ALLARDYCE, Author of 'Memoir of Admiral Lord
Keith, K.B.,' &c. With a Memoir by the Rev. W. K. R. BEDFORD. In two
vols. 8vo. Illustrated with Etchings and other Engravings. £2, 12s. 6d.

SIM. Margaret Sim's Cookery. With an Introduction by L. B.
WALFORD, Author of 'Mr Smith: A Part of His Life,' &c. Crown 8vo, 5s.

SKELTON. Maitland of Lethington; and the Scotland of Mary
Stuart. A History. By JOHN SKELTON, C.B., LL.D. Author of 'The Essays
of Shirley.' Demy 8vo. 2 vols., 28s.

SMITH. Thorndale; or, The Conflict of Opinions. By WILLIAM
SMITH, Author of 'A Discourse on Ethics,'&c. New Edition. Cr. 8vo, 10s. 6d.

——— Gravenhurst; or, Thoughts on Good and Evil. Second
Edition, with Memoir of the Author. Crown 8vo, 8s.

——— The Story of William and Lucy Smith. Edited by
GEORGE MERRIAM. Large post 8vo, 12s. 6d.

SMITH. Memoir of the Families of M'Combie and Thoms.
Originally M'Intosh and M'Thomas. Compiled from History and Tradition.
By WILLIAM M'COMBIE SMITH. 8vo.

SMITH. Greek Testament Lessons for Colleges, Schools, and
Private Students, consisting chiefly of the Sermon on the Mount and the
Parables of our Lord. With Notes and Essays. By the Rev. J. HUNTER
SMITH, M.A., King Edward's School, Birmingham. Crown 8vo 6s.

SMITH. Writings by the Way. By JOHN CAMPBELL SMITH,
M.A., Sheriff-Substitute. Crown 8vo, 9s.

SMITH. The Secretary for Scotland. Being a Statement of the
Powers and Duties of the new Scottish Office. With a Short Historical
Introduction and numerous references to important Administrative Docu-
ments. By W. C. SMITH, LL.B., Advocate. 8vo. 6s.

SOLTERA. A Lady's Ride Across Spanish Honduras. By MARIA
SOLTERA. With Illustrations. Post 8vo, 12s. 6d.

SORLEY. The Ethics of Naturalism. Being the Shaw Fellowship
Lectures, 1884. By W. R. Sorley, M.A., Fellow of Trinity College, Cambridge,
and Examiner in Philosophy in the University of Edinburgh. Crown 8vo, 6s.

SPEEDY. Sport in the Highlands and Lowlands of Scotland with
Rod and Gun. By TOM SPEEDY. Second Edition, Revised and Enlarged. With
Illustrations by Lieut.-Gen. Hope Crealocke, C.B., C.M.G., and others. 8vo, 15s.

SPROTT. The Worship and Offices of the Church of Scotland.
By GEORGE W. SPROTT, D.D., Minister of North Berwick. Crown 8vo, 6s.

STAFFORD. How I Spent my Twentieth Year. Being a Record
of a Tour Round the World, 1886-87. By the MARCHIONESS OF STAFFORD.
With Illustrations. Third Edition, crown 8vo, 8s. 6d.

STARFORTH. Villa Residences and Farm Architecture: A Series
of Designs. By JOHN STARFORTH, Architect. 102 Engravings. Second Edition, medium 4to, £2, 17s. 6d.

STATISTICAL ACCOUNT OF SCOTLAND. Complete, with
Index, 15 vols. 8vo, £16, 16s.
Each County sold separately, with Title, Index, and Map, neatly bound in cloth,
forming a very valuable Manual to the Landowner, the Tenant, the Manufac-
turer, the Naturalist, the Tourist, &c.

In course of publication.

STEPHENS' BOOK OF THE FARM; detailing the Labours of
the Farmer, Farm-Steward, Ploughman, Shepherd, Hedger. Farm-Labourer,
Field-Worker, and Cattleman. Illustrated with numerous Portraits of Ani-
mals and Engravings of Implements. Fourth Edition. Revised, and in great
part rewritten by JAMES MACDONALD, of the 'Farming World,' &c., &c. As-
sisted by many of the leading agricultural authorities of the day. To be completed in Six Divisional Volumes.
[*Divisions I., II., and III., price 10s. 6d. each, now ready.*]

STEPHENS. The Book of Farm Buildings; their Arrangement and Construction. By Henry Stephens, F.R.S.E., Author of 'The Book of the Farm;' and Robert Scott Burn. Illustrated with 1045 Plates and Engravings. Large 8vo, uniform with 'The Book of the Farm,' &c. £1, 11s. 6d.

——— The Book of Farm Implements and Machines. By J. Slight and R. Scott Burn, Engineers. Edited by Henry Stephens. Large 8vo, uniform with 'The Book of the Farm,' £2, 2s.

STEVENSON. British Fungi. (Hymenomycetes.) By Rev. John Stevenson, Author of 'Mycologia Scotia,' Hon. Sec. Cryptogamic Society of Scotland. 2 vols. post 8vo, with Illustrations, price 12s. 6d. each. Vol. I. Agaricus—Bolbitius. Vol. II. Cortinarius—Dacrymyces.

STEWART. Advice to Purchasers of Horses. By John Stewart, V.S., Author of 'Stable Economy.' New Edition. 2s. 6d.

——— Stable Economy. A Treatise on the Management of Horses in relation to Stabling, Grooming, Feeding, Watering, and Working. By John Stewart, V.S. Seventh Edition, fcap. 8vo, 6s. 6d.

STODDART. Angling Songs. By Thomas Tod Stoddart. New Edition, with a Memoir by Anna M. Stoddart. Crown 8vo, 7s. 6d.

STORMONTH. Etymological and Pronouncing Dictionary of the English Language. Including a very Copious Selection of Scientific Terms. For Use in Schools and Colleges, and as a Book of General Reference. By the Rev. James Stormonth. The Pronunciation carefully Revised by the Rev. P. H. Phelp, M.A. Cantab. Tenth Edition, Revised throughout. Crown 8vo, pp. 800. 7s. 6d.

——— Dictionary of the English Language, Pronouncing, Etymological, and Explanatory. Revised by the Rev. P. H. Phelp. Library Edition. Imperial 8vo, handsomely bound in half morocco, 31s. 6d.

——— The School Etymological Dictionary and Word-Book. Fourth Edition. Fcap. 8vo, pp. 254. 2s.

STORY. Nero; A Historical Play. By W. W. Story, Author of 'Roba di Roma.' Fcap. 8vo, 6s.

——— Vallombrosa. Post 8vo, 5s.

——— He and She; or, A Poet's Portfolio. Fcap. 3s. 6d.

——— Poems. 2 vols. fcap., 7s. 6d.

——— Fiammetta. A Summer Idyl. Crown 8vo, 7s. 6d.

STRICKLAND. Life of Agnes Strickland. By her Sister. Post 8vo, with Portrait engraved on Steel, 12s. 6d.

STURGIS. John-a-Dreams. A Tale. By Julian Sturgis. New Edition, crown 8vo, 3s. 6d.

——— Little Comedies, Old and New. Crown 8vo, 7s. 6d.

SUTHERLAND. Handbook of Hardy Herbaceous and Alpine Flowers, for general Garden Decoration. Containing Descriptions of upwards of 1000 Species of Ornamental Hardy Perennial and Alpine Plants; along with Concise and Plain Instructions for their Propagation and Culture. By William Sutherland, Landscape Gardener; formerly Manager of the Herbaceous Department at Kew. Crown 8vo, 7s. 6d.

TAYLOR. The Story of My Life. By the late Colonel Meadows Taylor, Author of 'The Confessions of a Thug,' &c. &c. . Edited by his Daughter. New and cheaper Edition, being the Fourth. Crown 8vo, 6s.

THE BULL I' TH' THORN. A Romance. In 3 vols. Crown 8vo, 25s. 6d.

THOLUCK. Hours of Christian Devotion. Translated from the German of A. Tholuck, D.D., Professor of Theology in the University of Halle. By the Rev. Robert Menzies, D.D. With a Preface written for this Translation by the Author. Second Edition, crown 8vo, 7s. 6d.

THOMSON. Handy Book of the Flower-Garden: being Practical Directions for the Propagation, Culture, and Arrangement of Plants in Flower-Gardens all the year round. With Engraved Plans. By David Thomson, Gardener to his Grace the Duke of Buccleuch, K.T., at Drumlanrig. Fourth and Cheaper Edition, crown 8vo, 5s.

THOMSON. The Handy Book of Fruit-Culture under Glass: being a series of Elaborate Practical Treatises on the Cultivation and Forcing of Pines, Vines, Peaches, Figs, Melons, Strawberries, and Cucumbers. With Engravings of Hothouses, &c., most suitable for the Cultivation and Forcing of these Fruits. By DAVID THOMSON, Gardener to his Grace the Duke of Buccleuch, K.T., at Drumlanrig. Second Ed. Cr. 8vo, with Engravings, 7s. 6d.

THOMSON. A Practical Treatise on the Cultivation of the Grape-Vine. By WILLIAM THOMSON, Tweed Vineyards. Ninth Edition, 8vo, 5s.

THOMSON. Cookery for the Sick and Convalescent. With Directions for the Preparation of Poultices, Fomentations, &c. By BARBARA THOMSON. Fcap. 8vo, 1s. 6d.

THOTH. A Romance. Third Edition. Crown 8vo, 4s. 6d.
By the Same Author.
A DREAMER OF DREAMS. A Modern Romance. Second Edition. Crown 8vo, 6s.

TOM CRINGLE'S LOG. A New Edition, with Illustrations. Crown 8vo, cloth gilt, 5s. Cheap Edition, 2s.

TRANSACTIONS OF THE HIGHLAND AND AGRICUL-TURAL SOCIETY OF SCOTLAND. Published annually, price 5s.

TULLOCH. Rational Theology and Christian Philosophy in England in the Seventeenth Century. By JOHN TULLOCH, D.D., Principal of St Mary's College in the University of St Andrews; and one of her Majesty's Chaplains in Ordinary in Scotland. Second Edition. 2 vols. 8vo, 16s.

———— Modern Theories in Philosophy and Religion. 8vo, 15s.

———— Luther, and other Leaders of the Reformation. Third Edition, enlarged. Crown 8vo, 3s. 6d.

———— Memoir of Principal Tulloch, D.D., LL.D. By Mrs OLIPHANT, Author of 'Life of Edward Irving.' Third and Cheaper Edition. 8vo, with Portrait. 7s. 6d.

TWO STORIES OF THE SEEN AND THE UNSEEN. 'THE OPEN DOOR,' 'OLD LADY MARY.' Crown 8vo, cloth, 2s. 6d.

VEITCH. Institutes of Logic. By JOHN VEITCH, LL.D., Professor of Logic and Rhetoric in the University of Glasgow. Post 8vo, 12s. 6d.

———— The Feeling for Nature in Scottish Poetry. From the Earliest Times to the Present Day. 2 vols. fcap. 8vo, in roxburghe binding. 15s.

———— Merlin and Other Poems. Fcap. 8vo. 4s. 6d.

———— Knowing and Being. Essays in Philosophy. First Series. Crown 8vo, 5s.

VIRGIL. The Æneid of Virgil. Translated in English Blank Verse by G. K. RICKARDS, M.A., and Lord RAVENSWORTH. 2 vols. fcap. 8vo, 10s.

WALFORD. A Stiff-Necked Generation. By L. B. WALFORD, Author of 'Mr Smith,' &c. Cheap Edition. Crown 8vo, 6s.

———— Four Biographies from 'Blackwood': Jane Taylor, Hannah More, Elizabeth Fry, Mary Somerville. Crown 8vo, 5s.

WARREN'S (SAMUEL) WORKS:—
Diary of a Late Physician. Cloth, 2s. 6d.; boards, 2s.
Ten Thousand A-Year. Cloth, 3s. 6d.; boards, 2s. 6d.
Now and Then. The Lily and the Bee. Intellectual and Moral Development of the Present Age. 4s. 6d.
Essays: Critical, Imaginative, and Juridical. 5s.

WARREN. The Five Books of the Psalms. With Marginal Notes. By Rev. SAMUEL L. WARREN, Rector of Esher, Surrey; late Fellow, Dean, and Divinity Lecturer, Wadham College, Oxford. Crown 8vo, 5s.

WEBSTER. The Angler and the Loop-Rod. By DAVID WEBSTER. Crown 8vo, with Illustrations, 7s. 6d.

WELLINGTON. Wellington Prize Essays on "the System of Field Manœuvres best adapted for enabling our Troops to meet a Continental Army." Edited by Lieut.-General Sir EDWARD BRUCE HAMLEY, K.C.B. 8vo, 12s. 6d.

WENLEY. Socrates and Christ: A Study in the Philosophy of Religion. By R. M. WENLEY, M.A., Lecturer on Mental and Moral Philosophy in Queen Margaret College, Glasgow; Examiner in Philosophy in he University of Glasgow. Crown 8vo, 6s.

WERNER. A Visit to Stanley's Rear-Guard at Major Barttelot's Camp on the Aruhwimi. With an Account of River-Life on the Congo. By J. R. WERNER, F.R.G.S., Engineer, late in the Service of the Etat Independant du Congo. With Maps, Portraits and other Illustrations. 8vo. 16s.

WESTMINSTER ASSEMBLY. Minutes of the Westminster Assembly, while engaged in preparing their Directory for Church Government, Confession of Faith, and Catechisms (November 1644 to March 1649). Edited by the Rev. Professor ALEX. T. MITCHELL, of St Andrews, and the Rev. JOHN STRUTHERS, LL.D. With a Historical and Critical Introduction by Professor Mitchell. 8vo, 15s.

WHITE. The Eighteen Christian Centuries. By the Rev. JAMES WHITE. Seventh Edition, post 8vo, with Index, 6s.

——— History of France, from the Earliest Times. Sixth Thousand, post 8vo, with Index, 6s.

WHITE. Archæological Sketches in Scotland—Kintyre and Knapdale. By Colonel T. P. WHITE, R.E., of the Ordnance Survey. With numerous Illustrations. 2 vols. folio, £4, 4s. Vol. I., Kintyre, sold separately, £2, 2s.

——— The Ordnance Survey of the United Kingdom. A Popular Account. Crown 8vo, 5s.

WILLIAMSON. Poems of Nature and Life. By DAVID R. WILLIAMSON, Minister of Kirkmaiden. Fcap. 8vo, 3s.

WILLS AND GREENE. Drawing-room Dramas for Children. By W. G. WILLS and the Hon. Mrs GREENE. Crown 8vo, 6s.

WILSON. Works of Professor Wilson. Edited by his Son-in-Law Professor FERRIER. 12 vols. crown 8vo, £2, 8s.

——— Christopher in his Sporting-Jacket. 2 vols., 8s.

——— Isle of Palms, City of the Plague, and other Poems. 4s.

——— Lights and Shadows of Scottish Life, and other Tales. 4s.

——— Essays, Critical and Imaginative. 4 vols., 16s.

——— The Noctes Ambrosianæ. 4 vols., 16s.

——— Homer and his Translators, and the Greek Drama. Crown 8vo, 4s.

WINGATE. Annie Weir, and other Poems. By DAVID WINGATE. Fcap. 8vo, 5s.

——— Lily Neil. A Poem. Crown 8vo, 4s. 6d.

WORDSWORTH. The Historical Plays of Shakspeare. With Introductions and Notes. By CHARLES WORDSWORTH, D.C.L., Bishop of S. Andrews. 3 vols. post 8vo, each price 7s. 6d.

WORSLEY. Poems and Translations. By PHILIP STANHOPE WORSLEY, M.A. Edited by EDWARD WORSLEY. Second Edition, enlarged. Fcap. 8vo, 6s.

YATE. England and Russia Face to Face in Asia. A Record of Travel with the Afghan Boundary Commission. By Captain A. C. YATE, Bombay Staff Corps. 8vo, with Maps and Illustrations, 21s.

YATE. Northern Afghanistan; or, Letters from the Afghan Boundary Commission. By Major C. E. Yate, C.S.I., C.M.G. Bombay Staff Corps, F.R.G.S. 8vo, with Maps. 18s.

YOUNG. A Story of Active Service in Foreign Lands. Compiled from letters sent home from South Africa, India, and China, 1856-1882. By Surgeon-General A. Graham Young, Author of 'Crimean Cracks.' Crown 8vo, Illustrated, 7s. 6d.

YULE. Fortification: for the Use of Officers in the Army, and Readers of Military History. By Col. YULE, Bengal Engineers. 8vo, with numerous Illustrations, 10s. 6d.

12/89.

www.ingramcontent.com/pod-product-compliance
Lightning Source LLC
Chambersburg PA
CBHW030129030726
47498CB00007B/2622